"My name is Car

There was a strange break in the middle of the words, almost as if he had suddenly changed his mind and decided not to tell her. But he finished the sentence smoothly enough, looking her straight in the eyes as he spoke.

"And I'm M—"

Her tongue stumbled thickly on the realization that she had been about to give away her real name. What if he knew who she was? She had no idea how long he had been in England. If he had read it in the local newspapers. She didn't want to take any chances.

"I'm Miss Jones," she said, and winced at just how prim and restrained it sounded. But it would do for now. After all, she had no way of knowing if he had even given her his real name.

"Pleased to meet you, Miss Jones…"

He gave the carefully formal name an ironic intonation, as if he was only too well aware of the way she was concealing the truth from him, but quite clearly he didn't care a bit.

Diablo. The name spun round inside her thoughts. *Diablo.* The devil. Carlos the devil. That sounded so ominous. Scary. But it was just a name, Martha reassured herself. Just his name.

The devil and Miss Jones. It sounded like a gothic romance.

KATE WALKER was born in Nottinghamshire, England, and grew up in a home where books were vitally important. Even before she could write she was making up stories. She can't remember a time when she wasn't scribbling away at something.

But everyone told her that she would never make a living as a writer, so instead she became a librarian. It was at the University College of Wales, Aberystwyth, that she met her husband, who was also studying at the college. They married and eventually moved to Lincolnshire, where she worked as a children's librarian until her son was born.

After three years of being a full-time housewife and mother she was ready for a new challenge, so she turned to her old love of writing. The first two novels she sent off to Harlequin Books were rejected, but the third attempt was successful. She can still remember the moment that a letter of acceptance arrived instead of the rejection slip she had been dreading. But the moment she really realized that she was a published author was when copies of her first book, *The Chalk Line,* arrived just in time to be one of her best Christmas presents ever.

Kate is often asked if she's a romantic person because she writes romances. Her answer is that if being romantic means caring about other people enough to make that extra special effort for them, then, yes, she is.

Kate loves to hear from her fans. You can contact her through her website at www.kate-walker.com or email her at kate@kate-walker.com.

Other titles by Kate Walker available in ebook format:

Harlequin Presents® Extra

THE DEVIL AND MISS JONES

KATE WALKER

~ Return of the Rebels ~

TORONTO NEW YORK LONDON
AMSTERDAM PARIS SYDNEY HAMBURG
STOCKHOLM ATHENS TOKYO MILAN MADRID
PRAGUE WARSAW BUDAPEST AUCKLAND

Recycling programs
for this product may
not exist in your area.

ISBN-13: 978-0-373-52862-2

THE DEVIL AND MISS JONES

THE DEVIL AND
MISS JONES

CHAPTER ONE

'WHAT the devil…!'

He had to be imagining things, Carlos Ortega told himself. He couldn't actually be seeing what was ahead of him.

Easing up on the throttle, he slowed the powerful motorbike to an almost crawl that was far more suited to the narrow country lane he had originally been riding down at a speed that much better expressed the turmoil of his inner feelings and stared straight ahead, frowning. But no matter how he blinked or adjusted his vision, the sight remained the same. The same impossible, unbelievable image just ahead of him. One that set his bemused mind wandering down strange and over-imaginative paths and into crazy ideas.

He'd heard stories of local ghosts. His companions in the bar last night had been only too keen to regale him with them over a pint of beer. This road, the villagers said, was haunted. By a bride who had been left at the altar, and had died broken-hearted, pining away for the man she had once loved but who had deserted her so cruelly. At least, that was the way that the traditional story went.

Not that Carlos believed in any such thing. The small, sleepy backwater of a place he had stayed in for the past couple of days was obviously riddled with stories and superstitions, some of which had been amusing enough last night while propping up the bar in the black-beamed old-fashioned inn where he had been staying. But now?

'No way!'

He found he was shaking his head inside his crash helmet and almost laughing as he had done last night when they had first fed him the story, obviously thinking they needed to earn the drinks he had bought them.

He'd gone down to the bar from his room because for the first time in a long while he'd wanted company. He'd moved from the point of being alone and finding that that was the way he wanted things to be after all that had happened, to feeling strangely lonely, which wasn't something he'd expected. He was used to his own company and he had, after all, come here deliberately to be on his own, to get away from the mess he had left behind him. He had wanted to be as far away from that—as far away from home as possible.

Home. Argentina wasn't any sort of home to him, but then, where was? It had hit with a wrenching jolt that there was now nowhere in the world he could call home. Oh, he had houses of course, several of them in the most expensive and exclusive parts of the world, and any one of them he would be happy to live in. But none of them was where he had any roots; where he thought he truly belonged. Where his family...

'Hah! *Family!*' His laugh was harsh, raw.

What family? He didn't have any family any more.

Everything he had thought was his had been taken away from him at a blow. And the only thing he had been left with was his mother. His lying, cheating, unfaithful mother. The mother who had made him a bastard right from birth and who had never wanted him in her life after that. He didn't even know who he was any more. His whole life had apparently been a fiction, his background, his ancestry, turning into a lie in the space of the time it had taken his grandfather to tell him the truth. A truth that had left him with precisely nothing of everything he had once valued, and once thought was what made him who he was.

So the stories he'd heard had been an amusement, a distraction from feelings he wasn't used to dealing with. They'd helped him pass an unexpectedly restless evening. But this morning in the very cold light of an early April day, belief in ghosts, ghouls and things that went bump in the night was very far from his mind.

And yet...

The freezing fog was shrouding the edges of the road in swirling shadows, occasionally drifting to obscure the vision on the grass verge on the left-hand side. It came and went so that he was forced to blink hard to clear his vision and make sure there actually was anything up ahead.

And it—*she*—was still there.

A woman. Tall, curvaceous, pale. Hair a rich honey gold—what he could see of it through the mist. And because it was pulled up in some ornate style on top of her hair, most of it was covered by the filmy veil—white like the ankle-length dress—that covered her face and fell down her back. Her arms were bare, as were her shoulders, the pale skin almost as white as the fitted bodice that shaped her high, rounded breasts.

A *bride*?

The figure of a bride, in full wedding regalia. Just as in the legend of the ghostly bride that had formed part of the evening's entertainment in the bar. But this was definitely no ghost because this particular bride was standing at the side of the road—incongruously clutching a bright blue very modern handbag.

And with her thumb raised in the time honoured gesture of someone hitching a lift.

'What the…?'

This time he slowed the bike to a complete halt, coming to a careful stop just a short distance away from the woman.

'Oh, thank God!

The voice was real. Not just something he had heard in his imagination or inside his head. Soft and slightly husky, it sent a shiver through him that had nothing to do with the paranormal ideas he had been conjuring up just moments before. A response that was all to do with the very real world. And the soft rustle of her silken skirts as she hurried towards him was not the silent drift of a spirit that didn't actually exist but very clearly made by something totally physical.

So just what the devil was she doing here?

'Oh, thank God!'

The cry escaped Martha's lips involuntarily, pushed

from her by the sheer disbelieving delight of seeing the motorbike pull to a halt at the side of the road.

'At last!'

At last she was not alone. At last someone else was in the same place as her. Someone—a man—a big man from the size and shape of him—had appeared on the road that had been empty and isolated for almost too long to bear. Someone who might be able to help her and maybe even get her somewhere safe and *warm* before she actually froze. She was dangerously close to that already, she admitted to herself as just the effort of running towards him made the blood quicken in her veins, bringing stinging life to the toes she had feared might actually become iced to the ground.

Not for the first time she cursed the wild romantic impulse that had led to her choosing this isolated spot in which to hold her wedding. Of course, originally, the isolation had been everything she had wanted. The large stately home, set in its huge grounds, was miles from anywhere, and hopefully too far from civilisation and too hidden to attract the attention of the paparazzi or anyone else who had been trying to find out just who she was. When she had first seen Haskell Hall it had looked absolutely perfect. The wedding venue of her dreams. A fantasy come true. Here she could have her special day in total privacy and, after that, who cared if anyone who lived nearby ever found out why her life had changed so totally, so dramatically?

But the day she had seen the hall had been a bright, clear, crisp morning, with the sun high in a wide blue sky. The sweeping drive up to the big house had been clear of the mist that had swirled around it this morning, and the temperature had been a good ten degrees or more higher than the bitter chill that seemed to have crept into her bones, turning them to ice as she had trudged up the path towards the road.

It had never seemed such a long, long trek either, when she had first imagined the journey in a horse-drawn carriage that would take her from her fairy-tale wedding and off on the honeymoon of a lifetime, her new husband at her side. But that had been when she had only driven down it in the secure, warm confines of a sleek, powerful car, snugly wrapped in jeans and a cashmere sweater. She would give her soul to be able to wrap something like that around her right now and ease some of the chill that had made the last half an hour or more such sheer misery. Though the truth was that it was the coldness inside that was far worse even than the weather.

Back then, her feet had been comfy and protected inside soft leather boots, not the delicate satin, crystal-decorated slippers that were now totally soaked through and feeling like little more than sodden paper between her feet and the rough surface of the road. Her hair was damp and had started to slide out of the ornate style that had been created only an hour or so before, her carefully applied make-up running down her face, washed away by the rain as she ran down the drive.

And the man she had been planning on marrying was still somewhere back in the Hall, hastily erasing all evidence of the dirty, illicit passion he had just indulged in. A passion that he had never felt for her, except in his lies.

'Please stop...'

She couldn't get to her rescuer fast enough, almost tripping over her long skirts as she ran towards him.

Two cars had already rushed past her. She wasn't sure if the drivers had actually seen her or, having seen, had decided to put their foot down and rush past, the sight of a bedraggled, mud-splattered bride, miles from anywhere, just too much for them to cope with. And she'd stood there, her feet turning into blocks of ice, her hands going blue, the skin of her face stinging with the cold.

She had thought that today was to be the start of her happy ever after. But for that to happen, then Gavin would have had to be her prince, instead of the ugly toad he had turned out to be. She supposed it could have been worse. If she'd still been caught up in the fantasy of being in love—in love with the idea of being in love—then she could have had her heart shattered as well. But she'd already had second thoughts, and it seemed that her instincts had been working true. But all the same the vicious, cruel words she had heard had taken every last trace of her self-esteem, her sense of herself as a woman, and shattered it into tiny pieces.

The thrum of the motorbike's engine had her running headlong down the rutted road, suddenly fearful that this unexpected rescuer too would put his foot on the accelerator and speed away, abandoning her totally.

'Please—please don't go...'

'I'm not going anywhere.'

The voice, muffled slightly by the silver helmet he

wore, didn't sound quite English. Or perhaps that was because of the wind roaring in her ears, the racing of her heart in panic at the thought that he might be about to leave her alone again. She was so cold she couldn't think straight.

But at least he had switched off the engine on his bike, had swung his long leg over the machine so that he was standing, tall and dark—so tall!—in front of her.

'I promise I'm not going anywhere,' he repeated.

'Oh, thank heaven!' It was a fervent sigh, rather ruined by the way that her teeth chattered together on the last word. 'I...'

'What the hell happened to you?' he demanded, the rich dark voice rough with something she hoped was concern.

How much did she tell him? *What* did she tell him? It wasn't just the cold that had numbed her brain so that she couldn't think straight. In the moments that she had run to be near him, coming to a halt at his side, she had suddenly found that her mood had swung from relief and delight to a new and disturbing rush of something very different. A sense of apprehension mixed with a sharp, intense awareness of the simple fact that he was a man. A man whose powerful figure and strong frame suddenly made her heart lurch in a mind-spinning shock of response.

'No—wait!'

It was a command, sharp, autocratic, and she realised that he was unzipping the substantial leather jacket he wore with battered denim jeans and heavy black leather boots. Shrugging himself out of it, he moved closer.

'Here...'

He slung it around her shoulders, letting it settle like a thick black cape over the exposed skin, the soaked silk of her bodice.

'You're frozen.'

'U-understatement.'

It was all that Martha could manage and even then her voice shook on the words. She was beginning to feel as if she had lost contact with her mouth, her lips frozen stiff so that it was hard to speak. The shivers she had been fighting off suddenly returned in full force, driving her to tug the jacket tightly around her, huddling into it for comfort. It was still deliciously warm from his body and it smelled faintly of clean musky male skin, and some tangy cologne that unexpectedly made her heart skip a beat. The feeling of relief from the cold was overlaid with another, unexpected pulse of heat that had nothing to do with the jacket but was a stunning, unexpected sensual response.

'Th-thank you.'

She wasn't quite sure how she got the words out. The shock that ricocheted through her in that moment seemed to clear her head, bringing her up short. She had been so overjoyed to have help, to see some other human being out here in the wilds, to have someone actually *stop* to help, that she hadn't stopped to think—about anything. But right now she realised that thinking was what she had to do—and fast.

She didn't know this man from Adam. Had no idea who he was and why he had actually stopped. She was here in the middle of nowhere, alone, defenceless—

she couldn't even run if she wanted to with the narrow, sleek skirt of her dress clinging close around her legs and ankles. She had thought that it looked so elegant when she had first tried it on. She had even—wonder of wonders—felt almost beautiful when she had looked in the mirror of her room back in the Hall when she had got ready. Well, Gavin had taken that impression and crushed it beneath his heel just moments later.

Was it really just an hour or so before?

His cruelty had driven her out of the house in a desperate need to escape—first from the wedding that had turned into her idea of a personal sort of hell and now, possibly from this man—this stranger...

Did he even plan to help her?

All at once the rush of warmth and delight that had sizzled through her when she had first seen him ebbed away fast, leaving behind a sort of bruised, painful feeling. Still clutching the jacket around her, pulling it tighter than ever as a sort of protection against the way she was feeling, at the same time she knew a longing to tear it off and throw it from her as if accepting it had led her into reckless danger. Unable to think straight, she took a couple of hasty steps backwards, almost missing her footing on a rough patch of grass and turning her ankle sharply so that she cried out in shock and pain.

'Hey...'

The man's hands, big, strong, encased in black leather gloves, came out to catch her, pulling her upright when she almost fell. Supporting her easily, he shook his head.

'No—do not look at me like that.'

It was there again, that hint of something foreign—exotic—in his words. This time she was sure that it was not her hearing that was deceiving her, but very definitely the sound of some accent that was nothing like the local flat-vowelled burr. It was unexpected, somehow shockingly appealing.

'I have no intention of hurting you, I swear... Look—'

His free hand unfastened his helmet swiftly. As he pulled it off he shook his head sharply, freeing the rather long jet black hair that was now exposed. The wind howled round them, blowing it against his face so that as he turned back to her he had to toss it out of his eyes.

And what eyes! Martha didn't know what she had been expecting. She could see so little of him, with his long body, those powerful hands, all encased in black leather and denim, his face hidden under the silver helmet. But from the hint of skin she could just see— golden, olive-toned skin that was not the pallid white of an Englishman at the tag end of winter—and the trace of accent she realised that she had anticipated something dark, deep brown or maybe a polished jet. Instead she found herself looking into a pair of mossy green eyes, glinting with the light of a many-faceted jewel stone that made them deep and dark while at the same time shot through with an almost golden hue. They gleamed above high, slanting cheekbones, fringed with impossibly long, lush black lashes that should have looked effeminate on a man but that somehow, in this strongly carved, stunning face just looked amazing—and incredibly, gorgeously sexy.

But he also looked dangerous. Big and dark and powerful. Those impossibly long, lush eyelashes should have softened his face, but instead they somehow contrasted so sharply with the high, carved cheekbones, the square, forceful jaw and uncompromising mouth that the impression they left was one of concealment, hiding the beauty of those stunning green eyes behind their dark fringe, and turning it into something secret, inscrutable—disturbing.

Just who was this man who had come to her rescue—knight in shining armour or the devil himself?

'Believe me, I have no intention of hurting you.'

He repeated the words with an added edge for emphasis and while they relieved her tension, that double edge to them had exactly the opposite effect. That accent didn't help either. It was too foreign, too exotic, to belong in any sort of world where she lived.

'How do I know that?'

He sighed, tossed back an overlong strand of hair that the wind had blown against his face. As she watched that sensual mouth twitch in something that might have been amusement—or an acknowledgement of her right to indignation—she felt a twisting bite of response that had nothing to do with unease and everything to do with a purely female reaction to a glorious specimen of manhood.

The problem was that it was not usually the way she felt about the opposite sex. The way she had ever felt about any man…even Gavin. That was one of the things that had made her face the fact that she was deluding herself about her proposed marriage.

'I can give you my word.'

'And what exactly will that mean to me?'

Once awoken, her sense of self-preservation had coming rushing back in double force. If she hadn't learned anything about the way that since her life had changed, everyone would react so differently towards her, then surely the devastating scene she had witnessed back at the Hall would finally—finally have taught her that she needed to take so much more care with relationships from now on.

But surprisingly, the memory of the sight that had met her eyes as she had walked into Cindy's room was having the strangest effect on her. Just when it should have made her stop and think, should have pushed her to have second and then very probably third thoughts about what she was doing, instead it seemed to have exactly the opposite effect. When she should have thought extra carefully and played things cautiously, sensibly, in the way that she had lived most of her life up to now, she suddenly felt that what she actually wanted was to break free, be less constrained. Sensible was very definitely *not* what she wanted to be.

Her life had been turned on its head. It had been blasted apart and there was no way she was ever going to be able to put the pieces back together again. At least not in a way that rebuilt the picture as it had been before. She had tried the safe, the careful—the damn *sensible*—and look where it had got her. Out here on an exposed moor, wearing a bridal dress for a wedding that had never meant a single thing that she had believed in. A future that had been a mistake from the start.

'What good is your word to me when I don't know who you are? Or anything about you.'

The look he shot her gleamed with challenge, a touch of dark humour flaring gold in those amazing eyes, reminding her that the truth was that she was in no real position to argue.

'You know that I am probably your only chance of getting to where you need to be—or back to wherever you came from.'

His cool gaze swept along the deserted road, the rain soaked hills surrounding them.

'Do you see a couple of hundred other cars—other bikes—queuing up to come to your rescue?' he drawled sardonically. 'To take you wherever you want to go?'

'There'll be someone else along…'

Even as she flung the words at him she knew that she was risking making a big mistake; cutting off her nose to spite her very cold and miserable face. His sceptical sidelong glance questioned her sanity in that statement just at the same moment as her own thoughts demanded to know if she was losing her mind.

'Fine,' he said, the single word curt and harsh. 'Have it your own way.'

He turned away from her, towards his bike, putting a couple of strides between them, the silver helmet swinging from its strap at his side. The gesture was so obviously meant to show that he was calling her bluff that the sparks of irritation it ignited held her silent even as she knew she was risking possibly her last chance of rescue. She could challenge him too, and she would even if her stretched nerves screamed at her that this was crazy, that she was risking being abandoned again. But he couldn't do that—could he?

But it seemed that he could as his long legs and powerful stride took him further from her, leaving her with only a view of his strong, straight back, those wide shoulders encased in tautly stretched white cotton, the black hair blowing wildly in the wind.

Indecision tore at her, making her feel raw and uneasy. Surely if he actually meant to do her harm then he wouldn't just walk away like this? If only she had brought her mobile phone with her—but she'd left that on the dressing table in her bedroom at the Hall, forgetting to put it into her handbag at the last minute.

'Wait…' she tried, low and uncertain, but the wind whipped away the sound of her voice, scattering it across the deserted hillside.

He had only got a few metres away from her and yet already she felt shockingly lost and alone. The leather of his jacket seemed to have lost some of its protection against the wind, and she was gripped by a terrible sense of fear at the thought of being alone again. It had been bad enough before but she suddenly knew that it would be terribly, frighteningly worse this time after the brief spell of human contact that this man had provided.

'Wait!' she tried again, louder this time.

She saw his determined footsteps slow, come to a gradual but definite halt. He didn't turn, but he *had* stopped, and the way that her heart lurched told her how important that was. Safe or not, her mind was made up.

'What time is it?'

It was perhaps the last question he had been anticipating, and as he turned the quick dark frown that drew
his black brows together told her that. But he turned
a quick glance at the workmanlike watch on a heavy
leather strap around his strong-boned wrist and then
brought his eyes back to her face.

'Almost two o'clock—is that important?' His gaze
and his tone had sharpened on the last words.

Her reaction had given her away. The start she had
been unable to suppress, the way that her breath had
hissed in through her teeth at the thought of the way
her day should have been going right now.

'Might have been,' was all she could manage.

It should have been the beginning of her new life.
The start of what she had foolishly believed was the
happiness she had been looking for for so long. She
might have turned up at Gavin's door to tell him that
she thought she was making a mistake, but the things
she had heard and seen had stopped her dead, unable to
deliver her message. And Gavin had been so intent on
his own sensual pleasure that he hadn't even heard the
door open. So he would have no idea the wedding was
not going ahead and if it was nearly two o'clock then
the ceremony she had run from was officially about to
begin.

'Will you help me? Can we get out of here?' A rather
wild gesture of her hand indicated the sleek, powerful
black and silver motorbike that stood at the side of the
road. 'On that.'

She had to get as far away as possible from the Hall
where no doubt there must now be a search in progress,

everyone wondering what had happened to the bride who seemed to have disappeared into thin air.

'I take it that you need to get to your wedding?' he asked now.

'Oh, no!'

She couldn't hold back on the horror that flooded her mind at just the thought of it. She could still hear those words, muttered in the thick rough tones of sexual passion.

'It's worth putting up with her in my bed—taking her much prized and held-onto virginity to be legally and fully her husband. Just think, darling—half of seven million when we get a quickie divorce—that's worth consummating the damn marriage with Miss Prim, even if I do have to lie back and think of the money. Maybe that will turn me on because she sure as hell doesn't. She's so big, it'll be like sleeping with a horse...'

'No way! That's the last thing I want!'

She'd shocked him so that his dark head went back, his amazing eyes widening for a second before narrowing again in swift assessment. Her nerves twisted painfully as she saw his frown.

'I—I want nothing to do with my wedding,' she declared, the bitter truth ironing out the shake in her voice. 'It would have been the worst possible mistake I could make so I—got out of there fast. Leaving it all behind me. And I want it to stay behind me—as far behind me as possible.'

'Es que la verdad?'

The slow drawl had a faintly mocking edge to it, one

that had her tensing every muscle as she nerved herself for his next comment. His next question—inevitably it would be something on the lines of exactly what she had left behind and why. And she wasn't ready to answer that.

'What language is that?' she asked sharply. 'Are you—Spanish?'

She'd asked something that had sparked a new mood in him, one that seemed to have a shade coming down over his eyes, hiding their expression from her. But now she was intrigued, wanting to know more.

'Argentinian, actually.'

'And what do you do there?'

Somehow she'd stepped over a line that he didn't want crossing and his response was brusque, dismissive.

'Horses and wine.'

So, a gambler? Or a breeder? A drinker or... She didn't know how to phrase the question and his stony face did nothing to encourage her to go further.

'You—you're a long way from home.'

'A very long way,' he agreed, his tone sombre in a way that made her feel he was talking of so much more than a physical distance.

'So are you on holiday—or—?'

The rough shake of his head, sending that wild wet hair flying, had her cutting off the question sharply.

'It seems that really we're two of a kind,' he said slowly.

There was a touch of dark amusement in his words, but there was also something more than that. Something that swirled, harsh and disturbing, at the bottom of his voice.

'How so?' Her voice caught sharply on the words.

That deep green gaze swept over her in cool assessment then swung back to his motorbike, eyes narrowed against the rain.

'We both just took off—turned our backs, left everything behind. Two of a kind.'

CHAPTER TWO

Two of a kind?

Just the thought of it took her breath away. It was true that was exactly what she'd done. She had felt that there was no other possible opening before her. But *him*?

Look at him! Did he look like someone in despair at anything? A man who had felt the need to walk, leave everything behind? A man who had lost...?

No, *lost* was the last thing he looked. Even with the drizzling rain misting his hair so that it hung damp around his face, the black strands whirled into crazy disarray by the wind, and the white cotton of his tee shirt plastered against the honed lines of his torso, the powerful ribcage, taut muscles, disturbed, or even dishevelled were the last words that came to mind to describe him. Strong, powerful, determined, totally in control fitted him better.

'You can't have!' Disbelief rang in her voice.

'And why not?'

It was flung at her and the flash of danger in his eyes held a warning that made her take a couple of hasty steps back and away. She had needed this sharp reminder that he was a total stranger and one she didn't know whether she dared to trust or not.

'But—don't you have a job—a home—family who care for you?'

'I have no home in Argentina now.'

It was a flat, hard statement, and it was only when it died from his eyes, leaving them bleak and opaque, that she realised there had actually been a light in the green depths, one that had made them warmer than ever before. And now she had driven it away with her foolish words.

'No family either.'

'I'm sorry...I didn't mean...' she began again, but he lifted his shoulders in a shrug that dismissed her concern. He deliberately switched on a smile but it was such a brief, on-off flash of a thing that it had no real warmth or even meaning. And that 'now' had had a special emphasis, one that made it plain the loss was of a recent date.

'Perhaps we're more alike than you'd think—both on the run, leaving our pasts behind.'

'Is that really what you're doing?' She couldn't see him running from anything.

But when she looked into those moss-coloured eyes she saw a shadow that swirled in their depths, giving them a look that she recognised. It was the expression that had been on her own face when she had looked in the mirror that morning and known that she was making a terrible mistake. That she couldn't go through with the wedding to Gavin. It was the expression of someone who knew they had burned their boats and for whom life could never be the same again. And it was carefully masked so that only someone who had been through the same thing would see past the determined defences.

'Everything?'

His laugh was harsh, dark, seeming to splinter in the damp-laden air like a glass that had been dropped on the stony, wet ground.

'Take a look around you.'

The wide, vicious gesture embraced the empty, rain-swept road, the parked motorbike.

'Right now what you see is what you get,' he declared.

'That's *all* you have?' she managed, on a very different note from the question she had asked before.

That dark head, the dishevelled overlong hair now soaked by the misty drizzle and clinging to the strong bones of his skull, nodded twice, hard, and undisputable.

'That's everything,' he agreed. 'A few changes of clothes, some bits and pieces in that bag, and what I stand up in. That's it.'

'But you… Why…?' she began hesitantly but this time he shook his head with a touch of impatience.

'I could ask the same of you,' he said and she was relieved to see that at last a trace of lightness had crept into his voice, making it much less frightening, more reassuring. 'But what would be the point? We're just strangers, two ships passing in the night. So let's leave the questions unasked. The whys unsaid.'

'Not even names? If I'm supposed to head off out of

here with you then you could at least give me a name to use.'

A shrug of those powerful shoulders conceded that point to her.

'OK…'

He took a step towards her, pulling off one glove and holding out his hand to her.

'My name is Carlos…Carlos Diablo.'

There was a strange break in the middle of the words, almost as if he had suddenly changed his mind and decided not to tell her. But he finished the sentence smoothly enough, looking her straight in the eyes as he spoke.

Diablo. The word spun round inside her thoughts. *Diablo.* The devil. Carlos the devil. That sounded so ominous. But it was just a name, Martha reassured herself. Nothing but a name.

'And I'm M…'

Her tongue stumbled thickly on the realisation that she had been about to give away her real name. What if he knew who she was? About the money she had won—the millions that had been all that had attracted Gavin to her. She had no idea how long he had been in England; if he had read it in the newspapers. She didn't want to take any chances.

'I'm Miss Jones,' she said, and winced at just how prim and restrained it sounded. But it would do for now. After all, she had no way of knowing if he had even given her his real name.

'I am pleased to meet you—Miss Jones…'

He gave the carefully formal name an ironic intonation as if he was only too well aware of the way that she was concealing the truth from him, but quite clearly he didn't care a bit.

The devil and Miss Jones. It sounded like a gothic romance. Or some blues song.

That hand was still between them, long and brown and strong and totally steady, totally dependable. Surprisingly it put Martha's mind at ease and had her moving to put her fingers into his, feel them swallowed up in the heat and hardness, the strength and—yes and the comfort of it.

She was totally unprepared for the effect that just that simple gesture had on her. Her hand touched his, warm skin against warm skin, and suddenly it was as if she were in the middle of an electrical storm as sensation fizzed along every nerve. It was more than warmth, more than contact, and heaven knew she needed both of those. It was something deep and primitive, wild and dangerous and yet somehow essential to life. It swept away the chill that had pervaded her body as she'd stood, miserable and lost, at the side of the road and it threatened to splinter her mind into tiny pieces as she fought to get her much-needed control back again.

Suddenly Martha knew a crazy, irrational need to go somewhere—anywhere—with this man—this Diablo. And not just because she wanted to escape from all she had left behind her, but because she wanted to go forward into something new and different—and startlingly exciting.

When she looked up into his face she saw something change there too. A whole new expression suddenly

came over his features, softening them, changing them
in the most dramatic way. His eyes warmed so that their
shadowed green now looked like the colour of the fields
where the rainclouds had parted and let the rays of the
sun shine through, illuminating them. And his mouth—
dear heaven, how sensual was that mouth? It was firm
and strong but the fullness of the lower lip gave it a
sexy curve that made something tingle right through
her body, particularly when he let a tiny hint of a smile
curl at the corners just for a moment. His grip on her
hand tightened, briefly, conveying a message of support and encouragement that she was anxious enough
to welcome hungrily. She even let herself wonder just
for one brief heady moment just what it might feel to
have that mouth on hers, feel it caress her skin.

'So now can we get on?' he asked. 'I don't know
about you but I'm getting tired of standing here in this
wind, getting soaked.'

'Of course!' Guilt at the way she had kept him hanging around, the rain soaking into his hair and shirt,
made her sound over-enthusiastic. 'But how do I get
on that—in this?'

Her gesture took in the long white silk skirt, sleek
and clinging at the waist, hips, around her legs, with
just the tiniest flare of material at her ankles. Her delicate veil, soft and flowing when she had put it on an
hour or so before, now hung limp and weighted with
rain around her face and head.

'I'm not sure I can manage it.'

Why did women wear those skin-tight skirts? Carlos
wondered. He was surprised that she could even walk

in that dress, let alone do anything else. It was sexy as hell though, in the way that it shaped her breasts, exposing just a hint of creamy cleavage, the suggestion of seduction so much more enticing than a full-on plunging neckline. The silk then clung to the swell of her hips, taking the eye down the length of her body to the point where the flounces of material kicked out around the knees. Was there anything more calculated to emphasise the womanly shape, the curves that some—mostly other women, he suspected—might consider to be rather fuller and more lush than current fashion demanded?

Not him. He liked a woman to be a woman and that meant that she had to have a female shape. And this Miss Jones certainly was all woman.

'We're going to have to do something about that.'

She hadn't expected to walk very far in the designer dress, he reminded himself. Only down the aisle... Just what the hell had happened to make her run out on her wedding? The need to know was like an itch in his mind though he didn't feel that she would be prepared to answer if he questioned her about it. Not the woman who only gave her name as 'Miss Jones'. So what was she so determined to hold back on? What did she have to hide?

And what sort of a groom would be fool enough to let a beautiful woman like this slip through his fingers when she had already agreed to marry him?

'And what would that "something" we have to do be? How exactly do you expect to manage...?'

'Easy,' Carlos drawled. 'Nothing to it.'

He had enough experience of getting women out of

their clothes to have some understanding of how female garments worked. Admittedly, the women concerned had been only too eager to help him. He had never had to plan on dealing with a woman's clothing so that he could help her run away from another man.

But from his memory of dealing with silk dresses in the past, they offered little resistance to strong hands. Just how hard could it be to get rid of some of that unwanted material?

'Leave it to me.'

In a moment he was on his knees on the wet road at her feet, long brown hands reaching for her dress, tanned skin dark against the pale material. He gathered it into his fingers, twisting, bunching slightly so that it pulled against her legs, making her take an awkward step back and then forwards again, forced to stay where she was, held prisoner by his firm grip.

'Just stay there,' he muttered, a note of command in his tone, one that made her freeze where she stood.

But the small movement she'd made had been enough to make him freeze too—though in a very different sort of reaction. In the same moment that she'd stepped back and forward he had bunched the fine silk of her skirt in his hands, lifting it ready to get rid of the constricting skirt. And that had exposed the slender length of her legs.

Infierno! She was actually wearing stockings and suspenders, the nervous twitch of her body taking the skirt up higher so that the delicate pale blue lace of a garter too was exposed. Clinging round the top of her thigh. For a couple of heart-thudding seconds Carlos's throat dried shockingly, his hands tightening in the slippery material.

'Stand still!'

His voice was gruffer this time, and he didn't care if she thought he was ordering her around. The struggle for control of his own senses, his own body, had put the rough note into his tone. This Miss Jones was one of those women who believed that the pulse point at the back of the knee was a good spot to spray some of her perfume. And she was damn right about that too if the heady, spicy scent that hit his nostrils was anything to go by. Not for Miss Jones the delicate floral perfume the lace and silk of her clothing and the fine blonde hair might suggest. Instead she wore something that spoke more of enticement, of sensuality. Obviously she had been planning on sharing that sexuality with the man she was supposed to have been marrying.

It was damned difficult to concentrate on what he was doing with his body hardening in instinctive response to the closeness of her delicate flesh, the scent of her skin combined with that sensuous perfume. A hot wave of jealousy of the unknown man she had planned to share this delectable body with tonight swept through him, making his fingers clench even more tightly on the white silk. He had to be a total fool to have let her get away—to have driven her away from him.

Well, maybe the fool's loss was his gain. Miss Jones as a prospective bride he would have had to leave well alone. This woman as a bride who had clearly had more than second thoughts about marrying the man she was promised to and who obviously wanted to put as much distance between her and her groom as possible was a very different matter.

'I said stand still!' he repeated as another twitch of her body brought that sexy scent to torment his senses all over again.

'I *am* standing still.'

Martha had to mutter the words between clenched teeth in order not to betray the way she was feeling. She just wished he would hurry up and get the job done as soon as possible. She didn't feel that she could take the screaming tension of her nerves and every one of her senses for many moments longer.

He wasn't actually touching her, only the material of her skirt, and yet the surface of her skin seemed to tingle as if he was actually stroking it, as if his breath was warm against her exposed flesh. The cold, miserable dampness of the afternoon seemed to evaporate in a second, leaving her body heated from the inside so that she felt sure that she would actually see steam rising from her clothes where the warmth dried them. But she couldn't drag her eyes away from the man at her feet. Looking down at his dark head as he bent over his task, her gaze was grabbed and held, drawn by a sensual magnetism, and her fingers actually twitched against her sides as she fought the impulse to reach out and touch, stroke the black, disordered strands back into smoothness against the strong bones of his skull.

She *wanted* to touch him. No, it was more than a want—it was something close to a need. She had to feel him, make some physical contact—something more than just the warm, strong comfort of his palm on hers, her hand held safely inside his. And yet she knew she had to hold back, because if she gave in to this wild, irrational need, broke through the natural, instinctive restraints that held them separate, then some intuitive feeling warned that it would never stay that way.

There would have to be more. She just knew it. No other man had ever made her feel this way. But what if he found her as unattractive as Gavin had done?

...even if I do have to lie back and think of the money. Maybe that will turn me on because she sure as hell doesn't. She's so big, it'll be like sleeping with a horse...

She couldn't bear it if another man found her so unappealing. It would be like presenting the other cheek after someone had slapped her viciously already.

As if sensing her thoughts Carlos suddenly paused, turned his head, and looked up, straight into her eyes. A burn like a bolt of lightning went straight through her as she saw the new darkness in that green gaze. A darkness that mirrored the way she was feeling, the stinging sensitivity that flooded every nerve.

And that was too much. Already way off balance with all that had happened that day, she could barely cope with her own response. The prospect of having to cope with the fact that he might be feeling something of the same was more than she could handle. For a moment the world seemed to swing round her, the ground rocking beneath her feet and making her feel desperately insecure. In a panic she actually stamped her foot hard on the wet surface of the road.

'What exactly are you doing?'

'This...' His response was as curt and raw-toned

as her own as he turned his attention back to the task in hand.

She felt a sharp tug, heard a faint sound of something ripping and suddenly there was a rush of cold air around her ankles, her calves. She wasn't quite sure what he had done until she saw him toss the white frill of silk to one side, having ripped it right off the bottom of her dress. Now she could move more easily. She could walk, might even be able to clamber onto that powerful beast of a bike.

'Thanks—'

Testing, tentative, she took a step towards it—another—then froze, another thought stilling her feet.

If she got onto that bike then she would have to sit behind him. *Close* behind him. She would have to wrap her arms around that lean, tight waist, rest her chest, her breasts, against the broad, strong back, feel the heat of his body reaching hers. She would have to open her legs wide, spread them to accommodate…

'No!'

'What the hell now?'

Carlos was getting to his feet, wiping his hands down the taut length of his denim-covered thighs. The strange connection there had been between the two of them seemed to have evaporated in a rush and his voice held a thread of irritation that grated uncomfortably on her nerves.

'Lady, make your mind up. What is it?' he demanded again.

'I—I'm scared.' She couldn't bring herself to say

of what because she couldn't even start to explain it to herself.

'I'm a perfectly safe driver.'

'I'm sure you're a fantastic driver!'

But that didn't mean that she would feel *safe* with him anywhere. And… From nowhere came another thought. One that shook her right through to the very core of her being.

If she felt like this now, with this complete stranger, how could she ever have thought that Gavin was the man she wanted to marry? How could she have been so blind as to think she felt enough for him to say yes to his proposal?

But after three long lonely years of nursing her mother through her last illness, she had been looking for love—for a family—for a future. And she had fallen into his grasp like a ripe little plum. A ripe, stupid, easily deceived little plum. She had needed to be loved, had been in love with the idea of love. At least she had seen sense before it was too late.

'Isn't there a law about wearing a helmet on a motorbike?' she hedged, expecting and seeing his impatience at her reaction.

'I thought you wanted to get out of here.'

'I do—but only…'

'Only if you can do it legally…'

The mockery in his eyes and his tone was open now. And never before had she wanted so desperately to throw off her careful, conventional personality, cast caution to the wind and just go with what life offered her. Being careful had led to her engagement to Gavin and look where that had landed her. She shuddered at the thought of what might have happened if she hadn't seen sense...

What life offered her now was the chance to escape with this man, this *Diablo*. She should grab at it with both hands. But even as she opened her mouth to do just that Carlos had tossed his helmet towards her so that she only just caught it, managing to grab it before it hit the ground at her feet.

'Here—will that suit, *señorita*?'

The exasperation in his voice was making her see this situation from his point of view, and with that came a strong sense of the absurd. What must he have thought when he had come speeding down the road and seen her—a vision in white silk and lace, in jewelled slippers that were rapidly approaching the consistency of damp tissue paper? She'd chosen those slippers so that she didn't tower over Gavin, she recalled. There would be no such need with Carlos—he must be—what—five inches—more?—taller than her five feet eight.

'But,' Carlos continued, a hint of amusement lightening his tone, 'there is no way that helmet is going to fit over that...' He gestured towards the ornate hairstyle, the veil held in place by a delicate tiara.

'I know—so please...'

Meeting his eyes was a big mistake. With that new warmth in them, it only threatened to set off her thudding pulse all over again. Her heart kicked so hard in her chest that she felt sure he must see it under the fine silk, the delicate lace. And the rush of heat along her veins meant that her throat had dried painfully and somehow she couldn't swallow to relieve it.

'Do—do you think that you could help? Can you unfasten this thing?'

She lifted a hand to tug at the securely pinned veil.

'What am I—a lady's maid?' he muttered, but there was no harshness in his tone. And that disturbing gleam still burned in his eyes as he came closer.

'Just pull them out—get rid of them. If you can rip my dress to pieces then surely you can deal with some hairpins.'

A sudden shocking thrill shot through her at the thought of Carlos really ripping her dress to pieces, not just tearing off the flared skirt, and she could feel hot colour flood her face in response.

'*Por supuesto*... Let me see.'

She didn't know if it was to hold her still or to soothe her, ease away the nervous mood that was making every muscle taut with impatience, but unexpectedly he lifted a hand to her face. Softly, almost delicately, he cupped her cheek, curving his hard palm over the soft skin as he angled her head to one side, turning it so that it caught the best of what dull grey light there was.

And that action seemed to freeze her where she stood. In a day of shocks, confusion and bewilderment, the effect of that light, gentle touch was the most mind-blowing of all. It was warm and soothing, easing the restless stinging in her nerves and making her feel as if she were melting from the inside out. She wanted to turn her face into his hand, rest her cheek more firmly

against his palm and just let the feelings of tension
seep away.

She expected that those big hands would fumble with
the task before him. That at least he would tug at some
of the pins, twisting them free. She knew that she would
have done that herself, particularly if she was impatient to have the job done as she sensed that he was. He
might have himself carefully under control but there
was a tautness in the long powerful body next to hers
that communicated the fight he was having to do so.
She recognised it from the tension in her own body.

What was it he had said? That he had just taken off,
leaving everything behind. Leaving *what* behind? And
where? That accent didn't belong here on the moors of
the north of England. And the tanned olive skin, the
polished jet hair marked him out as someone as alien
to this landscape as if some sleek, powerful jaguar had
suddenly stalked the mist soaked hills. Just the thought
made her gasp in reaction.

'*Qué?*'

Carlos had caught the tiny indrawn breath, pausing
in this task, the deep green eyes going sharply to her
face and locking with her widened grey ones.

'Am I hurting you?'

'Oh, no. No.'

'Hurting' was not the word for what was happening
to her. She only knew that all the nerves in her stomach were tangling into tight, uncomfortable knots, and
the stinging sense of tension might have ebbed away
but only to be replaced by a new hot, tingling sensation, running like electricity over her skin. A yearning

that was uncoiling deep inside and that made her want to reach out to this man. Be closer to him. She wanted more of that touch. More of him.

'I want to get out of here.'

With you. She only dared let the words echo inside her head; too afraid, too unsure to actually let them out into the air. She didn't know what she would be unleashing if she did.

'So let's do this…'

Carlos's eyes locked with hers, lingering for a darkly revealing moment, before he bent his head again, turned his attention back to the task in hand. And it seemed that with each pin that was eased from her hair, tossed with the tiniest sound of metal hitting tarmac onto the road, something in her mood, her body, her whole life lightened and eased. She felt the knots untangling from her nerves, the tension leaving her muscles so that she could stand taller, straighter, easier. Something of the horror and the pain that had slashed at her soul seeped away, filling her with a new sense of anticipation and hope.

'So, your wedding—just why did you run out on it? What did this guy do to you?'

She didn't know if he was asking to distract her from the time it was taking to free her from the veil or because he really wanted to know but because she couldn't see his face and, more importantly, he couldn't see hers, she found it surprisingly easy to answer him.

'Why did I turn round and get out of these as fast as I could, never looking back?' she asked, trying to bring her chin up in defiance, adopt an I-couldn't-care-less attitude that she felt might not be fully convincing.

'You have to admit it's not the usual way these things go. Normally by this time the bride and groom would be…'

'Gazing into each other's eyes as they made their loving vows? So are you feeling sorry for my poor, deserted groom, now that his wife-to-be has run out on him? Well, don't—he'll be more than happy having hot, passionate sex with my chief bridesmaid—that is if he hasn't already exhausted himself shagging her on the bed we were supposed to have shared tonight.'

'The bastard did that?'

A blazing sense of outrage was like a wildfire in Carlos's voice and his hands tightened in her hair, twisting sharply so that she caught back a cry of pain. But in the same moment that she felt the small discomfort in her scalp, she also knew a sudden rush of relief mixed with a surprising bubble of unexpected delight. He cared enough to be angry at what Gavin had done. His outrage was like a balm to the wounds she'd carried with her from the Hall. Some of them at least.

'I walked in on him—on them—while they were hard at it. I walked out again pretty damn fast,' she added with brittle flippancy. 'I don't think they saw me—they were…totally absorbed. I managed to get out of the place without anyone seeing me and after that I just ran and never looked back.'

Until she had reached the road across the moor and, too tired and too cold and miserable to go any further in her stupid wedding finery, she had stopped on the verge and tried to hitch a ride.

She wasn't going to tell him the rest. She couldn't yet even bear to look at those other words for herself and take in just what Gavin had said. She hadn't even been a woman to him—not a real person, just a source of a future income.

'I'd like to deal with this snake. No man should treat a woman that way. You should let me take you back there.'

'And do what?' Martha challenged, finding the disgust in his voice almost too much to bear. 'Storm into the Hall, all guns blazing, and challenge him to a duel? No, thanks! That way everyone would know exactly why I'd pulled out of the wedding—just how badly humiliated I'd been—instead of just thinking I'd got cold feet at the last moment.'

A raw, bitter laugh bubbled up in her throat, almost choking her. She'd had pretty cold feet by the time he'd found her. She could swear that it was only now that they were fully thawed out.

'Which actually was the truth. And I'd much rather that Gavin think that I'd walked out on him *before* I found out how he'd been spending the hours before our wedding. He'll never know for sure whether I caught him with his pants down or not—'

And would never have the cruel satisfaction of knowing that she'd heard herself described as someone he would have to lie back and think of the money when he slept with her.

'That's definitely the way I prefer it. Besides I can

fight my own battles, thank you. I've been doing it for long enough.'

'How so? What about your family?'

'I don't have one. I never knew my father—he ran out on my mother as soon as he knew she was pregnant, so it was always just the two of us. Three years ago, Mum was diagnosed with liver cancer—she died last summer.'

And it had been in the aftermath of that loss that on an uncharacteristic impulse she had bought the winning lottery ticket that had changed her future. If only she could have done that earlier so that she could have made her mother's last months more comfortable. If only she hadn't spent those years isolated as her mother's carer so that she had no experience of life and men that might have helped her realise just what Gavin was up to, see past the pretty lies he told her.

'I'm sorry.'

His words were kind, as was his tone, but Martha still found that they made her tense in nervous apprehension. If he made a move towards her, if he touched her, perhaps tried to take her into his arms to express his sympathy, then she would shatter, go to pieces, and she had no idea how she would ever put herself back together again.

But perhaps something of her mood communicated itself to the man at her side. The sympathy she'd feared—dreaded—didn't come. Instead Carlos tossed one last pin away, completed his task and straightened up. The tiara dangled from one set of strong fingers, the veil clenched in the other hand. He held them out to her.

'There.'

With the new sensations buzzing inside her it felt almost as if she had been set free, released from something that was more than just the restrictions of the wedding finery. She'd hit the lowest point just hours before. And if that was the lowest point in her life then surely the only way was up.

'Now I can move on—leave it all behind me. You know, I'm not running away but going forward—getting away from what would have been a terrible mistake, starting again.'

She moved forward to take hold of them. But the new lightening of her mood pushed her feet further than she had anticipated, the lift in her spirits making her almost dance towards him. And suddenly she was on tiptoe, leaning forwards, reaching up to plant an impulsive kiss on the lean plane of his cheek.

'Thank you!'

And that was when everything changed. When it seemed as if the world stood still, the countryside freezing around her in the same moment that her breath stopped in her lungs. The birds in the trees stopped singing, the wind stilled in the branches, dropping into sudden silence. The skin of his face was cold and damp against her mouth, the taste of his skin suddenly intense and smoky against her tongue. She was frozen where she stood, looking up into his eyes so that she saw the sudden darkness in them, the way that the irises had expanded until there was only the tiniest line of deep green at the rim.

She read what was coming in those eyes. Read it and welcomed it, her heart kicking sharply against her rib-cage as she held her breath. She didn't have to wait long. His arms came round her, warm and tight, strong as steel bands, lifting her even further off the tarmac and crushing her firmly against the powerful toned shape of his chest. His head came down fast, his mouth coming over her own, hot and hard, demanding and power-ful. Her lips were crushed, parting slightly on a gasp of shocked response as she gave herself up to the pressure of that kiss.

She had never known anything like it, she recognised hazily, struggling to bring her thoughts under any sort of control. Never experienced a kiss—or a response—like this at any other time in her life. She had kissed, of course. Kissed and been kissed, but it had never been anything like this. And the caresses she had exchanged with Gavin had been like tepid water when compared with this deluge of red-hot lava swamping her, taking her control, her senses and her ability to think at all rationally with it. Her heart was pounding, her head whirling.

This was how she should feel when she wanted a man.

When a man wanted her? The thought piled another shock on shock.

'Belleza...' Carlos muttered roughly against her lips, her cheek, her throat as he took the kiss over her face, down her jaw, along her neck...

'*Diablo...*'

Somehow it was only his second name that came to her lips, the surname that suited him so much more than just Carlos. *Diablo*—the word that described him as much as it labelled him. Diablo—the devil—and he had all the seductive power and enchantment of the Prince of Darkness right now. The sensual temptation that could pull her right off the path she had been following—the path of common sense and sanity—and lead her straight down a newer, wilder route. One that offered her a chance to be a woman she had never been before.

How had she got to the age of twenty-three and never known sensations like this before? How could she have kissed before, been kissed and caressed before, *have imagined herself in love* when she had never experienced anything like this? Carlos's hard, demanding mouth worked a dark magic on her senses, stirring them into swirling, heated life that drove away the cold damp of the afternoon and set her blood racing in her veins. It was all she had never known and yet all she had ever wanted. And she *wanted* this. Wanted more of the sensations firing through her body. More of the sensual demand of those firm male lips, more of...

But at that moment her thoughts were stopped dead in their tracks, the heated moment destroyed in a heartbeat as a huge clap of thunder broke almost directly overhead, a torrential downpour following straight after. A torrential, icy downpour that swept away their heated ardour and soaked them through to the skin in seconds.

'Infierno!' Carlos swore, snatching his mouth away from Martha's. 'Let's get out of here!'

Grabbing her arm, he hurried her to the bike, their feet splashing in the water that was already creating a torrent along the road. Pausing only to place the helmet rather unceremoniously on top of her now loosened hair, he swung a long leg over the powerful machine and started the engine. Martha didn't allow herself any sort of second thoughts as she followed him, clambering up behind him a lot less elegantly and huddling up close to his long, powerful back.

'Hold on tight,' Carlos tossed at her, his words barely audible above the rain and the roar of the engine.

It was only when she moved to do just that that Martha realised she still held the tiara and the delicate veil, the latter now hanging like a damp rag from her fingers. As she looked down at them they seemed like rather shabby, damaged symbols of the life she had thought was going to be hers.

But not any more. She knew now that the life she had believed was ahead of her had been nothing but a fraud, a fake. Gavin had never loved her—he hadn't even wanted her. The only thing he had been after was the money she brought with her. She was well rid of him.

'Hang on!' Carlos said again, revving the engine impatiently. 'If you're coming with me.'

If you're coming with me. Martha's heart skipped a beat as she considered the question just for a second.

Of course she was going with him. Where else could she go? It wasn't just that Carlos Diablo offered her a way out of here, transport to help her run from her aborted wedding as far and as fast as she could manage. He also offered her the promise of a very different life. An exciting and adventurous way of living that she would have contemplated with a terrified horror just a few days ago. But now she was desperate to move on. She had taken the first step when she had taken a look at herself in her bridal finery and known, deep in her soul, that she was making a mistake. Her new-found courage had taken her to Gavin's room to tell him of her decision. What she had heard there had shaken her to her core, but perhaps it had been the jolt she had needed to drive her to put her past behind her, escape the careful, cautious persona her restricted life had trapped her in and embrace the woman she had felt herself to be when Carlos had kissed her.

'Ready?' he asked now and although she knew he couldn't see her she nodded her head in enthusiastic agreement.

'Ready!'

With a defiant gesture she tossed the pretty crystal tiara from her, not caring that it bounced and shattered into four small pieces as it hit the ground. The veil followed as she flung it with all the strength she could find, watching in satisfaction as it was caught by the wind and tossed about wildly, dancing far away from her across the fields. She thought she knew how it felt.

'I'm so ready!'

Flinging her arms around his narrow waist, she held on tight as the powerful motorbike roared off down the road. She couldn't imagine why she had ever felt worried about riding on the bike behind Carlos. Why the idea of sitting up so close, of holding on so tight had spooked her. Now that she was actually doing it, it felt like the most natural, the right thing to do. And the most exciting. The speed they were travelling at, the lash of rain against the visor of her helmet, the spray that was tossed up by the speeding wheels, were all shockingly, devastatingly exhilarating. There was an edge of danger there too, one that had her clinging on for dear life. But in spite of everything, she felt wonderfully safe, totally secure with the strength and power of Carlos Diablo to hold onto.

She didn't know where she was going and she didn't care. She only knew that she was heading away from the past, moving into a very different future, and that this man—this strong, sexy, gorgeous man—would be with her part of the way at least. She didn't know for how long but quite frankly that didn't matter. That was one good thing about having burned her boats completely—she could go wherever she wanted to and never look back. The marriage that would have been a dreadful mistake, the time of trying too hard to be in control, were all behind her. This wild, adrenaline-charged ride was her present. The future was ahead of her.

The one thing she knew was that after this she was going to go into that future putting herself first. She was through with being careful, controlled, restrained. She was giving up on playing it safe. There was a whole new world out there and she was going to discover it.

CHAPTER THREE

IT WAS the wildest ride she had ever been on. So smooth and so fast that it almost felt like flying. As if the motorcycle, under Carlos's skilled control, was soaring, diving, swirling through the air until she felt dizzy with excitement, her heart pounding wildly.

She had no idea at all how long they had been travelling, whether it was minutes, hours, or even more. She only knew that at some point the lashing rain stopped, a weak wavering sun finally appearing. But only for the last short section of the day. Before she had even had time to appreciate its brightness, that sun was fading out again, sinking down towards the horizon and taking the daylight with it. That was when the motor on the bike, so strong and reliable until now, suddenly started to cough and judder, sounding disturbingly rough as Carlos gradually slowed it down and brought it to a stop at the edge of the road.

'Something wrong?' Martha asked, seeing his frown as he tested the engine once again.

'I'm afraid so. We're not going to get much further on this tonight. It will need to be looked at in a garage.'

'Oh, no.'

She didn't even trouble to hide her disappointment. Was this the end of her leap into something new? That exciting future that she had been hoping for coming to a stuttering halt on a broken-down motorbike before it had even got started.

Carlos was looking round at their surroundings, the streets that were the start of the small town they had just reached.

'I'm sure this place must have a rail station—or a bus service. Something that can get you on your way.'

That would be the sensible way to handle things. The way the old Martha would have taken. This new Martha was prepared to take chances. And the chance she wanted to take was right here in front of her.

'But it's starting to get dark, and believe me I think I'm more than far enough away from what was going to be the biggest mistake of my life. I don't know about you but I could do with pausing for breath, taking stock. There must be some sort of a hotel or a B and B near here.'

'You want to stay overnight?'

Did he have to sound so under-enthusiastic? New Martha was having a real struggle to suppress Old Martha, who seemed determined to resurface, fighting her way through the chinks in New Martha's resolve. Carlos had already suggested putting her on a train or a bus—did she need any more evidence of the fact that he didn't feel about her the way she felt about him? Wasn't she just risking making a complete fool of herself? And she'd be so much better to take him up on the train station suggestion and get on her way before she did anything even more stupid.

Something of the wild exhilaration of the motorbike ride started to seep away and Gavin's cruel words came sneaking back into her mind. Was she really just deceiving herself in thinking there could be a new Martha? And yet there had been that kiss…

'OK—forget it—'

Somehow she managed to make her voice sound careless and unconcerned. She even managed a shrug of the shoulders to dismiss the suggestion as unimportant.

'No,' Carlos cut in sharply. 'A hotel is a very good idea.'

'Somewhere cheap,' Martha added hastily, suddenly concerned that his hesitation might have been because he—who had openly declared that 'what I stand up in' was all he had—might not be able to afford a stay somewhere that cost too much.

But Carlos wasn't listening.

'I think that we should find somewhere to stay as quickly as possible.'

'You do?'

Carlos made a gesture towards her head, still concealed by the protective helmet.

'Take that off,' he said, and for all that the words were low and calm they were an order, one that he clearly meant should be obeyed.

Which they were. Because Martha found that when he looked at her like that, dark deep green eyes staring down into her face, she didn't want to resist. She wanted to do exactly as he said. So she pulled off her helmet and shook her hair free, freezing as Carlos's hands stilled the movement, his dark head coming suddenly close and his mouth capturing hers.

It wasn't a hard, demanding kiss like the one out on the moors, the kiss that had come out of nowhere and sent her senses reeling in the space of a heartbeat. Compared with that it was almost gentle. But where the first kiss had started a wild fire of excitement deep inside, this one seemed to draw her in, switch her on, starting a slow, sensual spiral of heat that uncoiled in the pit of her stomach, spread through every nerve, every cell, until she felt sure that she must be glowing in the gathering dusk. Every inch of her skin felt awake and sensitised, her breathing unsteady as the beat of her heart. The taste of him on her lips, the swirl of his tongue against hers, were as intoxicating as some vintage brandy that warmed her deeply and sent her head spinning at the same time.

When Carlos pulled back, taking his lips from hers and straightening up, she couldn't hold back the faint moan of protest that escaped her at the sudden sense of loss. She found that she was swaying forward, losing balance, as if he had been holding her and had suddenly let go. But it was only when his hands came out to close over her arms, supporting her and keeping her upright, that she realised he had been keeping his distance all the time and she had been drawn towards him, like a needle to a magnet, by the pull of her own senses.

'Carlos…'

It was all that she could manage because simply

speaking brought her tongue into connection with her lips, tasting him there all over again. Her hand crept up to cover her mouth, as if trying to keep his kisses there longer, press them deeper into her skin, and she felt his grip around her arms tighten as his eyes burned down into hers.

'I know…' he said, his voice low and rough-edged. 'I *know*. That's exactly how it makes me feel too. That's why we need to find somewhere to stay. The next time that I kiss you I might not be able to stop and we'd need to be inside—in the warm.'

In the warm and somewhere where we can take this further.

He didn't say the words but they were there in his eyes, in his tone, in the hands that still held her, the heat of his palms reaching through to her skin even through the barrier of the leather jacket. Vaguely, at the edges of her awareness, Martha knew that there were other people about, cars that swept past them on the road, but she didn't really notice them. All her attention was focused on the man before her, on that savagely handsome face, and the rest of the world seemed to have blurred into insignificance.

The next time that I kiss you… The words swung round and round in Martha's head.

So was she going to trust a complete stranger? A man she had met barely hours before? Was she going to go with him, find some hotel, simply because she wanted to?

Ah, but there was the answer. She *wanted* this. New Martha wanted it so much. The way that it had stabbed at her heart when it had seemed that Carlos was determined to put her on a train or a bus, part from her without looking back, told her just how much she wanted it. She had never felt more alive. Excitement was fizzing through her, fed by the long fast ride from the moors to here, the heat and hardness of Carlos's body pressed tight against hers.

She wanted more of that.

And as if to confirm her decision, the rain that had eased off for the last hour suddenly started again, coming down in a rush that drenched her hair in the space of a few seconds, soaking into Carlos's tee shirt and jeans so that they clung to the powerful lines of his body, defining taut muscles, hard ribcage, in a way that made Martha's mouth dry.

'Inside...' was all she could manage , dragging her eyes away and spinning round to see if she could spot anywhere they could head for. Across the road and a little further along, a lighted sign proclaimed a family hotel.

'Over there...'

Carlos took her hand as they hurried towards it, his warm, firm grip reminding her of the moment that he had given her his name and she had put her hand into his. That irrational moment of believing that she was safe with this man, that he would not hurt her, had influenced her thinking ever since. But wasn't it the truth that she was never going to let him hurt her? She was going into this with her eyes wide open. And she wasn't looking for emotion—definitely not for love.

As for her earlier fears that he might not want her, if

the way he held her hand now was anything to go by, Carlos had no intention of letting her go any time soon. He didn't so much lead her as steer her firmly in the direction he wanted to go and she had little option but to go with him. But she didn't want to pull away. Right at this moment all she wanted was to stay like this, with her hand in his, his strong body shielding her from the worst of the rainstorm—and from the emotional storm that had turned her life inside out earlier this afternoon.

A few moments later, with the bike left in a section of the small car park, they headed towards the brightly lit doorway.

'Let's hope they have a room,' Carlos said. But then he swung back to face her again, one eyebrow quirking up in enquiry. 'Cheap enough?'

'What? Oh—yes…'

She had forgotten that out of concern for him she had stipulated that they should find a cheap B and B and she hadn't really expected the question to be turned round onto her. Briefly she wondered what he would think if she told him that what was in her bank account would probably allow her to buy the place outright and still have plenty of change.

But that was the sort of thing she wasn't prepared to share with him. Not yet, perhaps not ever. She'd be every sort of a fool if she let him believe that she was anything other than some ordinary girl who had got cold feet at the thought of her wedding. So far he had only reacted to her as the Miss Jones that he had met so unexpectedly and had rescued from the disaster she had left behind her—and that was exactly how she wanted it. Especially when this dark and devastatingly striking man made it obvious that he was attracted to her almost as much as she was to him.

'Absolutely fine. Oh!'

Her response was cut off sharply on a cry of shock. The uneven ground was positively the last straw for her battered and soaked satin shoes. The heels slid one way, her feet another, there was a ripping sound as the delicate fabric finally gave way and split all the way down the sides. With a shocked cry Martha flung out her arms, fighting to regain her balance, her whole body tensed in nervous anticipation of landing hard on the cold, wet cobbles.

It didn't happen. Just as she lost her footing completely Carlos moved, strong arms coming out to catch her, haul her up before she hit the ground. With what seemed like barely any effort he swung her up into his arms and held her tight, one arm firm around her waist, the other supporting her thighs.

'Let's get you inside.'

Kicking the ruined shoes out of the way, he carried her up the steps and through the main door into the warmth and light of the reception. There, he ignored the stunned gape on the face of the woman behind the desk as he strode straight up to her, Martha still in his arms.

'The sign outside says that you have vacancies.'

Was it because she was held so close to him, her head resting against the broad chest, that his accent had never sounded richer, sexier? Martha wondered. Certainly the receptionist thought so as her amazed expression changed to one of eagerness to please.

'Of course, sir.' She turned her most winning smile on the man before her, completely ignoring Martha in his arms. 'What were you looking for?'

What *was* he looking for? Suddenly Martha found herself swinging between two opposing emotions, not knowing which one to go with. Held like this against the hard, taut ribcage, her head resting just above his heart, the musky scent of his skin tantalising her nostrils, she felt the burn of excitement sting its way through her body. If she turned just a little she could press her lips against the lean, tanned column of his neck, taste his skin as she had done when he had kissed her. She wanted more of his kisses, more of him. Just being held by him was making the heat pool between her thighs. But—her heart skipped several beats at the thought of being alone with this man—this stranger—behind closed doors, in a bedroom.

The receptionist was pressing keys on her computer as she spoke and Carlos took the opportunity to lower his head so that his mouth was close to Martha's ear, his warm breath feathering over it, brushing her damp hair aside.

'One room or two?' he muttered, soft and urgent, so low that there was no chance that the receptionist would have caught the question.

As it was Martha was not quite sure she had heard right. Had he really said…? Looking up sharply, she found her gaze locked with the dark intensity of his and knew that he *had* asked the question. He was giving her the choice—and that whatever she decided, he would go with. The realisation was so freeing that the rush of relief was like a blow to her head.

That and the realisation that he didn't care who she was or what money she had. She was just someone he had met—and was overwhelmingly attracted to. All he wanted was *her*.

'One,' she whispered back, then, feeling that the quiet word didn't quite say enough, didn't express the way she was feeling, she lifted her head and turned her face to the receptionist.

'A double room,' she said, calm and clear, and felt the strong steady beat of Carlos's heart jerk hard under her cheek, revealing without words the way he felt about her decision.

More keys on the computer clicked, and Martha turned back to Carlos, lifting her head to look him in the eyes.

'You can let me down now,' she told him. 'I can walk…'

But he shook his head adamantly, totally rejecting her suggestion.

'No way, *querida*,' he murmured, obviously not caring who heard him this time. 'I've been waiting to get my hands on you for too long—I'm not letting go now.'

Finally taking possession of their room key, he rewarded the receptionist with a devastating smile, then, hooking his small travel bag over his wrist, he carried Martha towards the lift. She was painfully aware of the way that his actions, combined with their dishevelled appearance, had made them the focus for the stares of almost everyone else in the hotel entrance.

'Let me go!' she snapped at him, feeling her cheeks burn fierily in embarrassment. 'Put me down!'

'I said, no way.' Carlos turned a wicked smile on her, totally unperturbed by her wriggling attempt to get free. It only provoked him into holding her tighter, making her pulse pound even harder.

'But everyone's looking.'

'Let them look,' he returned totally unperturbed. 'Now press the button for the lift, *querida*. The sooner I get you upstairs, the better.'

'Carlos!' Martha protested weakly, but she pressed the button as instructed, knowing that her only way out of this public spectacle was to allow him to get her into the privacy of the lift.

Luckily it arrived quickly and she was carried into the small cubicle. Now at last Carlos let Martha slip down to the floor, deliberately controlling the action so that she slithered all the way down his body, held so close that she was pressed against every firm inch of him, the white silk of her dress sticking to the damp cotton and denim he wore. The heat that was generated between them was more than physical, the pulse that throbbed through Martha's veins making her imagine that there must be steam rising from their soaked clothes as a result.

A moment later he had manoeuvred her into the corner. With her back pressed up against the metal wall, he placed one hand on each side of her head, holding her face just where he wanted it. And then he kissed her again. Kissed her long and deep, a soul-draining kiss that weakened her knees, set her head spinning. Kissed her so thoroughly that she felt she was actually swooning under the sensual magic he worked on her. Heat and hunger were uncoiling deep inside her, melting her bones and making her yearn for things she had never experienced before.

Her arms came up around his neck, fingers tangling in the dark damp strands of his hair, holding him close as her mouth opened under his to deepen and prolong the kiss, her tongue dancing with his as she gave herself up to the wonderful sensations that were flowing through her. She pressed herself close, feeling the heated evidence of his desire for her against her pelvis, and knew a kick of real excitement at the thought that her needs were mirrored in his powerful body. Mirrored and equalled if the sigh that escaped between their lips when she swayed against him was anything to go by.

'Carlos…' It was both a sound of delight and a cry of yearning. 'I want…' Deliberately she stroked herself against him and laughed in delight as she heard his breath catch in his throat.

'Belleza. Bruja.'

Strong hands seared their way down her body, smoothing over her shoulders under the leather jacket, pushing it halfway down her arms, exposing the creamy swell of her breasts, the valley between them, to his burning gaze.

'Bruja?' Martha questioned breathlessly. 'What?'

'Witch—temptress!' he translated roughly, his voice thickened with need, his broad palms curving around the warm weight, cupping it and lifting it towards his mouth. 'How can you be like this now, when you know I have to wait…?'

His growled protest was interrupted by the lift coming to a halt at their floor, the doors sliding apart, reminding them that they were about to be revealed to anyone who was waiting to head downstairs. Luckily the corridor was empty, but one look at Carlos's disconcerted expression had Martha laughing out loud.

'So much for "let them look",' she teased. 'I swear you'd have been mortified if anyone had been there.'

She deflected the make-believe glare he shot her with a wide smile, loving the way that this powerful man was suddenly putty in her hands and all she had to do was be herself.

'Only because they might have delayed our arrival in our room,' Carlos shot back. 'But as it is—you see we no longer have to wait…'

Once more he swept her off her feet, hauling her up into his arms as he set off down the deserted corridor. And Martha flung her arms around his neck and held on tight, pulling his face towards her for hungry, snatching kisses, making it impossible for him to see and throwing him off balance so that he banged into the wall, first on one side and then the other, time and again, his attention distracted by taking the opportunity to kiss her back.

'*Querida*…' It was a sound of breathless, raw protest. 'How am I to know which room…?'

'What number is it?'

'305…'

Martha dragged her attention away from Carlos's sexy mouth for long enough to look around her.

'Here...'

It took a moment or two's fumbling to find the key card, insert it in the lock. But then they were in and hurrying over the deep red carpet in impatient need to reach the bed. His canvas holdall went one way onto the floor, her handbag another, and then Martha tumbled onto the cream satin covers, Carlos coming down almost on top of her, his lips still crushing hers, one foot coming out to kick the door closed behind them. His attention was solely focused on kissing, touching, caressing.

Her hair was splayed out around her head and he tangled his fingers in it, crooning something in rough Spanish as he lifted it to his mouth and kissed the silky strands. Then he combed it down, smoothing it over her shoulders, over her breasts, and his caresses followed the same path, making Martha squirm in heightened response, her head going back against the pillows, her neck arched as if to invite his kisses more.

'I have wanted to do this since that first moment I saw you. Wanted to touch you here...' Long bronzed fingers stroked her cheek. 'And here...'

The pressure of his touch smoothed over the swell of her breasts, heat burning through the fine white silk to make her gasp out loud.

'If you knew how much self-control I needed when I tore that ridiculous frill from your dress—when really I wanted to do this...'

The offending skirts were pushed aside and upwards,

those tormenting fingers following the same path, skimming up her thighs to the place where the fine lace of her stockings ended and the warm soft flesh was exposed. His hands traced soft, erotic patterns on the exposed skin while at the same time his tormenting mouth moved lower, over the curves of her breast exposed by the neckline of her dress.

She was melting inside—melting or burning up, Martha didn't know which. She only knew that the touch of his hands, his hot mouth on her skin, had broken the storm that had been waiting to happen from the moment they had first met. It was like being swamped by a tidal wave, heated sensual delights crashing over her in a wild force that stopped her thinking and left her only capable of responding.

And she just wanted to touch him. She couldn't keep her own hands still, wanted to explore the long, lean body that pressed her into the softness of the bed. She traced the straight, strong back, the sculpted torso, let her fingers tighten over the corded muscles in his arms, feeling their force move and tauten underneath the warm satin of his skin. The white tee shirt had pulled up from his waist and she could let her hands slide underneath, tracing the line of his belt.

His mouth was at her breast now, kissing her through the soft silk, and the heat and damp created by his lips were a new stinging force of erotic sensation against the tightened nipples that pushed against the lacy confines of her bra.

'Carlos…'

She moved restlessly beneath him, her body straining against his, her head moving restlessly on the pillow. The scent of his body was all around her, warm and musky and spiced with the perfume of desire that was more intoxicating, more arousing than any of the most carefully created, most expensive fragrances.

From behind her closed eyes she felt those wicked fingers tugging at the tiny pair of knickers that were all that came between him and her most intimate core. Tugging them aside, he stroked beneath, brushing lightly over the heated bud that was the centre of the most erotic sensations. When she moaned her response aloud he closed his hands over the elastic and lace confection and tugged it down her legs, exposing her completely to him.

'You too...' Martha spoke roughly, reaching for the buckle on Carlos's belt and tugging at it, her fingers shaking so that she was having very little effect.

'Un momento.'

Carlos laid his hand across hers to still the restless movement, making her eyes fly open in concern. He was only inches away. Green eyes so dark they were almost black as they looked deep into hers. She could see the glaze of desire that clouded them but for some reason—some inexplicable reason—he was holding back. And it was costing him—the lines of strain around his unsmiling mouth told her that.

And that revealing tension made her heart kick in excitement at the thought that she could have this effect on such a man. He could actually suffer such frustration—because of her.

Nervously she licked dry lips.

'Is something wrong?'

'We have a problem. No protection—I have no condoms. I—wasn't expecting this.'

'Neither was I…'

No condoms. She heard the words but her mind almost refused to accept it. Her body, buzzing with pleasure and burning up in arousal, certainly did. Dear heaven, they couldn't stop now! She felt she would die, or at the very least break apart, shattering into tiny pieces, if they had to try and impose restraint now.

The she remembered, looking round hazily for her handbag.

'My bag… There's some there.'

Gavin had insisted. Of course he hadn't wanted children. Not with her. But Gavin was the past and Carlos was very much in the present. Her ex-fiancé had made her feel as if she had nothing to offer a man—unless it was the fortune she had won by sheer stroke of luck. Carlos, by contrast, made her feel all woman, wonderful, special—he made her feel desirable.

He made her feel wanted. And he was what she wanted. What she wanted was right here, in this hotel room, and if it was for one night only then that would be enough for her. She wouldn't ask for anything more.

'I have condoms in my bag.'

She waved towards where the bag lay on the floor where she had dropped it as they came inside. Carlos jackknifed up and off the bed, stooping to snatch it up. He opened it roughly, looked inside, found the packet she meant quite easily. She had barely time to feel the loss of the warmth of his body before he was back with her, long frame covering her, heat flooding her once again as his lips kissed their way along the arched line of her neck.

'*Belleza*...' he muttered against her throat, the warmth of his breath tracing the word along her skin.

'What does that mean?' The words slipped past her control, wanting—needing it to mean what she thought.

'*Belleza*—you are beautiful.' Carlos lifted his dark head sharply. 'You doubt me?'

How could she doubt him when she saw that look in his eyes, the darkness that burned away all the mossy green and left only the deep black that seemed to draw her in?

'You are beautiful too,' she managed through lips as dry as paper. 'You make me want…'

A hot rush of embarrassment swept over her, drowning her, taking her words from her. How could she come right out and say it?

'So tell me what you really want.' It was a command, low and compelling, and she knew that it was now or never.

'You know!' But it was obvious that he wasn't going to let her off the hook. She was going to have to do this herself. 'I want you to kiss me.'

'You only had to ask…'

His hand came under her chin, lifted her face towards his and his mouth touched hers, his lips just brushing the sensitive skin very softly.

'Like that?' he questioned, his words just a breath that blended with hers.

'No.' It was a sound of protest. 'Not like that—and you know it.'

'Oh, do I?'

The thread of faint laughter through the words was her undoing, knocking down her defences in a way that no other, more forceful, approach could ever do. She found she was reaching up, offering him her mouth again, trying so hard to catch the warmth of his kisses as they danced in the air above her, just out of reach.

'Then show me—let me know what you had in mind.'

There was no mistaking that this time the green eyes glowed with the flame of temptation, of warm enticement mixed with a hint of challenge. If she wanted him, the look that burned deep into her eyes said, then she was going to have to show it. And, oh, she wanted him.

'I meant this…'

Lifting her head, she pressed her mouth against his cheek, tasting the smoky flavour of his skin, feeling the rough edge of his stubble making her lips tingle, stinging her tongue faintly when she let it slide over the darkness shading his jaw.

'And this…'

She let her kisses move upwards, slowly, enticingly, approaching the corner of his mouth with slow, deliberate provocation. He held himself completely still— too still—so that she knew he was holding back his own response, fighting for control. And the way that a single muscle jerked in his cheek told her how close he was to losing it even if he was determined not to show it. Her heart thundered wildly at the thought that she

had such power over him. It was a heady sensation that
blended with the yearning need that burned low down in
her own body to make her feel as if she were balanced
on the edge of a high, dangerous precipice, coming so
very close to tumbling right over the edge. But if she
was going to fall, she was taking Carlos with her.

'And this…'

She wanted to take his mouth with her own, to feed
her passion with the taste of him, but he had moved before she had a chance and his lips crushed hers, opening
her to him, plundering deep, demanding, instead of giving. Her head spun, her senses swam and she found she
was clinging to him, hands closed over the hard bones
of his shoulders, fingers digging into the tight muscles
as her legs lost all strength and gave way beneath her,
making her sag against him.

'I want…' she tried but the words were driven back
down her throat by another of those almost brutal kisses
in the same moment that she was swung off her feet
and lifted onto the bed.

'My turn,' Carlos muttered against her throat, trailing
that hot, tormenting mouth over skin that was already
on fire with need for his kisses, his touch. 'I want you
naked beneath me, open—hungry…'

Even as he was lowering her onto the bed his hands
were busy at her back, finding the delicate zip, sliding
it down so that the front of her dress gaped loose, exposing her breasts and the scented valley between them.
His mouth kissed its way down the creamy slopes, lick-
ing, nibbling, even occasionally nipping at the fine skin

in a way that made her throw back her head and moan aloud.

'Carlos ...' she choked his name out, her own hand scrabbling at the hem of his tee shirt, pushing it aside so that she could indulge the demanding need to touch his skin, feel his muscles bunch and flex under her fingertips.

But a moment later, when he tore open the silk of her dress, exposing the fine lace of her bra against which her pink nipples were straining in hungry demand and bent his dark head to take one rosy peak into his mouth, suckling hard, even the thought of his real name vanished from her mind. Instead it was the other name he had given her that came to her lips, the name that seemed more—more fitting, right somehow.

'Diablo...' she muttered, rough and urgent. 'Oh, Diablo.'

It was as if the sound of her voice had broken into the passion that had him in its grip. For the space of a thundering heartbeat he paused, lifting his head and looking deep into her eyes. She saw the glaze of hunger in his eyes, the burn of colour across the slash of his cheekbones.

'I'm not in this for the long term. I can't promise you for ever.'

She almost laughed aloud, amazed that he would even think she cared. She couldn't imagine for ever. Could only think of *now*.

'I'm not looking for for ever,' she managed unevenly. 'All I care about is now.'

And reaching up, she took his mouth with hers again,

kissing away his need to speak, leaving him incapable of forming any words as her seeking hands found the buckle to his belt, tugging it loose and snatching at the button on the denim waistband. His erection strained under her touch and when she tugged the zip down it sprang, hot and hard, into her waiting fingers.

'*Madre de...*' Carlos groaned as he felt her hand close around him.

'Now...' she repeated, emphasising the word with all the need that was like a burn in her blood, branding her as his without any hope of salvation. 'Now...'

'Protection...'

Somehow he managed to think beyond the immediate, something she was incapable of managing, and a hurried, near frantic grab brought the packet of condoms into reach after what seemed like an eternity of wait but was actually only the space of a few seconds.

'Hurry...'

She was reaching for him, wanting to help him, but in fact only complicating matters and making him fumble, rip the foil packet roughly. With a muttered curse, shaking his head violently, he pushed her aside so as to do the task himself. But at last he was sheathed and settling between her welcoming thighs, the heated pressure of his arousal edging very close to her yearning, hungry core.

'These have to go...'

The fine silk of her underwear ripped in two as he pulled it aside, knowing fingers stroking the damp folds, the throbbing nub that was already so sensitised, her whole body convulsed in pleasure at his lightest touch.

'No more,' she gasped. 'Not like this. Don't keep me waiting…now…'

'Now…' he echoed, thick and rough, raising himself on his elbows, angling his powerful body so that he could drive into her, sheathing his length in one long, forceful thrust.

She had thought that she was ready. She should have been ready. She was already half out of her mind with wanting him, needing him, hungering for him. Her body was open to him, achingly prepared, and so was her mind. She had readied herself, she *wanted* this so desperately, that she had thought she would be able to bluff this out, show no sign that this was her first time.

But when she felt the length and power of him filling her so completely, even as she welcomed it, gloried in it, there was one tiny part of her heart that missed a beat, a tiny flicker of reaction that she just couldn't hide. Her body betrayed her, stiffening, clenching, and to her horror she saw Carlos stiffen too, felt his mouth still at her breast, his head lift so slightly. She could feel his tension mounting, his passion ebbing. Something was wrong. Something had changed his mood completely.

'No…'

He couldn't stop. Couldn't withdraw. Not now. Not ever…

Frantic fingers clenched in his hair, hauling his head up and close to hers. Clamping her lips on his, she silenced any protest he was about to make, and at the same time she opened her body even more to his, moving her hips so that he moaned a response into her mouth. Still holding his head with one hand, she trailed her other fingers down his long, straight spine, feeling his muscles tense, his powerful form jerk under her touch. His response was even more violent when she let her hand wander between them, stroking along towards the point where the two were joined together. She felt the heat and the hardness of him, her hand instinctively knowing how to touch, how to provoke, until he bucked hard against her, catching his breath harshly.

'Jones!' It was a raw, guttural exclamation.

'Diablo,' she echoed his tone. 'Don't stop now. Don't...'

'Stop?' He was clearly close to losing control, his tone was raw and rough, the single word followed by a string of violent curses in his native Spanish. 'Hellfire, lady, you ask too much of man...'

Reaching up, he grabbed at both of her hands, wrenching them away from their tormenting journey over his body and flinging them up onto the pillow, one either side of her head, where he held her fast. Powerful fingers clamped bruisingly around her wrist. Just for a moment wild, passion-burned eyes glared down into Martha's wide grey ones and her stomach clenched in a volatile blend of excitement and terror at the thought of what she had unleashed.

'This is what you want... You asked for this—and believe me, lady, you are going to get it.'

Still keeping her prisoner, he let his mouth plunder first one breast and then another, drawing the pebbled nipple inside mouth and suckling on it deeply, even scraping his teeth gently over the surface so that she writhed in frantic response. And all the time he used his body, his knowledge of lovemaking with consummate skill, knowing just how to move, to stroke in and out, to twist so slightly until his heat and hardness rubbed against the centre of her yearning need with the most devastating effect.

She felt as if she were adrift on a wild, heated sea of sensuality, drifting in whatever way the current would take her, with no will or thought of her own. Warm waves drowned her, taking her with them so that she was lost in a world of aching pleasure and yearning, hungry need such as she had never imagined could ever exist before. She was surrounded by Carlos, the musky, intimate scent of his arousal, the taste of his skin, the burn of his mouth, the soft brush of his hair against her sensitised flesh. She was at the mercy of sensations she had never dreamed could even exist before, very definitely going down for the third time, and carless of where it would take her.

Then just as she thought she would drown she felt a new and stunning sensation, a pulsing heat, the wildest drumming of her heart, her nerves, that built and built until she was almost screaming with the tension that stretched her body tight, lifting, yearning, reaching… reaching for something she didn't know…

'Let go, Jones,' Carlos grated in her ear, his breath hot on her skin. 'Let go and give yourself to me. Come for me, *querida*…come, *mi ángel*…'

One more powerful thrust, one more touch of his mouth on the most sensitive skin of her breast and she was flying, high into the stars, losing herself completely with a sharp, wild cry of surrender and delight. She could no longer see or feel, only experience, only give herself up to the blazing delight that took her completely out of herself. The only other thing she was aware of was the way that a shaken, blistering heartbeat or two later Carlos too gave a tortured groan and she knew the flood of his heat inside her as he joined her in the wild, soaring flight to ecstasy.

CHAPTER FOUR

MARTHA knew that she had to come down eventually. For one thing her over-sensitised body couldn't take any more of the blazing sensations that had burned it up, blowing her mind. She felt that she couldn't stay at this peak of heightened sensitivity and still live. So slowly, slowly, she felt the sizzling pleasure ebb away, leaving her nerves with an ache of reaction that was close to being bruised. Gradually her breathing eased, her frantic heart rate slowed and, gulping in air, blinking hard, she gradually found that she was sinking back down to earth, back to reality, finding herself, at last lying still and exhausted, totally drained, under the heavy, limp, abandoned weight of Carlos's sated and exhausted form.

She knew he was there by the heat and the weight of him, but she didn't dare to actually look him in the face, try to read just what he was thinking. The memory of the sudden stiffness in the long, hard body, the way that he had stilled before she had driven him beyond the limits of his control came back to haunt her now.

Had she done something wrong? Disappointed him somehow? She had no experience to go on so she had nothing to compare it to. No way of knowing if it had been as good for him as it had been for her. *Like sleeping with a horse...* From a dark corner of her mind Gavin's soul-destroying comments threatened to come crawling back and she frantically tried to push them away.

He had wanted her; it was that simple. He had wanted her and she—oh, she had wanted him so much. And that being so, there was no way at all that she could regret what had happened. How could she ever rue such a wonderfully glorious initiation into the reality of sex? She had never imagined that it could be anything like that. No matter what she had heard or read—it was so very very different to experience it.

And having experienced it, then surely no one could ever regret it. Could they? Not even Carlos?

She flinched inwardly as, as if he had caught the sound of his name in her thoughts, Carlos stirred suddenly, sighing deeply and rolling over to one side, off her, to land on his back on the bed.

'That was not supposed to happen,' he declared harshly.

So much for hoping he wouldn't regret it, Martha acknowledged miserably. If she had had any lingering hopes at all then that flat, cold, hard statement had sounded the death knell for all of them.

But of course she was forgetting one very important fact. Where she had nothing to compare what had just happened with anything, to Carlos it was just another experience, maybe no more or no less than anything else—quite probably less. Wouldn't a man like him want a sexual partner who could match him in knowledge and expertise? A woman who could give as good as she got, not some innocent who was lost in the wonder of it all and who had all but lost consciousness at the ecstasy of her first orgasm.

'You can say that…' A mean little rush of insecurity pushed the words from her lips, but even as she spoke them she knew they were a mistake. 'But I didn't exactly see you fighting it.'

Carlos's breath hissed in between clenched teeth, adding to her mental discomfort and making her nerves tie themselves into sharp painful knots in her stomach.

'You're right…'

In a rough, abrupt movement, he swung himself up into a sitting position to toss the condom into the bin, then turned away, sitting on the side of the bed with his back to her.

'I wasn't fighting it—and that was my worst mistake.'

Angrily he shook his dark head as if in despair at himself and Martha dug her teeth down into the softness of her lower lip, wondering if he knew just how much it hurt to hear him describe this way what had just happened between them—the glorious, totally special moments they had shared. No, not shared. The magical moments she had known—the loss of her virginity—he was now dismissing as 'my worst mistake'.

'I wanted it…'

She wasn't going to let him take the blame—damn it, she wasn't prepared to let anyone take the blame! As far as she was concerned there was no blame to be allocated. They were both adults, both consenting…

'And so did you...'

'I know damn well that you wanted it!'

Pushing himself upright, Carlos swung his legs over the side of the bed so that he was sitting turned away from her, the long straight line of his back turned towards her, the only thing she could see as he pushed his hands against his face, bronzed fingers digging into the bones of his skull.

'You made that only too plain,' he continued, raking both hands roughly through his hair in an expression of some emotion she couldn't begin to explain, not knowing whether it was anger, disgust or just plain fury at himself to have lost control so completely. She only knew that it was so very difficult to only be able to speak to his back, having no chance to look into his face, to try to read his expression in his eyes. 'The problem is that I have a personal rule. One you made me break.'

'Rule? What rule?' Martha whispered.

Her words spurred him into action, making him lurch up from the bed before whirling round to face her. The burn of dark rejection in his face had her flinching back against the pillows, her blood suddenly icy cold in her veins.

'You were a virgin.' He tossed it at her as if it were the worst possible accusation in the world. His face had suddenly closed up against her. His eyes were hooded, shuttered, and the tightness of his jaw spoke only too clearly of control he was imposing on his mood.

'And that was news to you?'

From the heated glow of sensuality, she now felt as

if someone had tossed a bowl of cold water over her, jolting her back to reality and awareness. And that feeling put the ice into her voice, into her expression as she faced him.

'What about the dress—the veil—?'

With hands that were very far from steady she gesticulated wildly at the white silk spread out around her on the satin coverings.

'Didn't they give you a clue?'

'Women wear white for a wedding even when it is not in the least appropriate.'

'So you didn't think it meant exactly what it says on the tin?' Martha cut in sharply, pain and bitter disappointment putting the question into the defiantly flippant form.

'*Qué?*' Carlos frowned darkly, not understanding her slang reference.

'You didn't think I might actually be entitled to wear white?'

This was not the time to reveal the way that the sensual perfume she wore had gone straight to his head—and to more basic parts of his anatomy—when he had torn that frill of silk from the bottom of her skirt, Carlos told himself. That it and her sensually voluptuous body had whispered of sex to him before he had known anything more about her. His pulse was still fighting to return to normal after the wild passion that had swept through him at the taste of her mouth, the feel of her skin. With the tight pink nipples pebbling against his tongue he hadn't been able to think of anything beyond the hunger that had thundered through him, let alone come to any rational conclusions about the sort of woman she was.

He had never wanted a woman as much as he had wanted this Miss Jones. All the more so because she had reacted to him only as Carlos Diablo. Just a man. She had no idea of his real background and the wealth that came with it.

And now with the appalling realisation that, not only had he broken his number one rule but that he had been so out of control, so knocked off balance that he hadn't been functioning as efficiently as possible when taking care of their protection and the damned condom had split battering at his thoughts, he couldn't think straight at all. His head ached with the possible implications, the repercussions that might follow.

When he had been a small boy, just after his father had died and his mother had gone away leaving him behind, he had had a recurring nightmare. He would be lying in bed—asleep but he didn't know it—and when he looked around him it seemed that the walls of the room were closing in on him, the ceiling coming down. He felt that way now, but he wasn't asleep, he was wide awake. The only other time that it had oppressed him had been when he was eighteen and when Ella—another damn virgin…

'Why didn't you think I was a virgin?' Martha demanded, breaking into his unwanted memories.

'You had been engaged. Most people these days are intimate before they legalise their relationship. You had condoms in your bag. And you didn't damn well behave like a virgin. I didn't suspect…'

'And if you had?'

If he had, then he would never have touched her. He would have put her on that train or the bus as he had originally planned and walked away, grateful for the freedom he needed. A freedom that it was not worth risking for the fleeting sexual satisfaction of a one night stand, no matter how much the blood that was still bubbling in his veins told him it had been so much worth it. The hungry ache in his body that was already demanding the pleasure of a repeat performance. That pleasure was too highly bought with all the ties that went with it.

He felt trapped; he couldn't breathe. But the worst part of it was knowing that it was his own stupid fault. His own stupid, lustful fault. He'd had more restraint when he was eighteen. Tonight he had been so out of control, so at the mercy of his hunger for this woman that he had neglected even to consider the bitter lessons of the past.

His brain had been so scrambled that he hadn't even remembered them. There hadn't been a space for them in his head at all.

But there was now, damn it.

'It's quite simple. I don't sleep with virgins.'

If she had felt cold before, Martha told herself, then now it was as if ice were forming in her veins. Her body still throbbed in the after effects of the passion she had thought they had shared, but Carlos showed no sign of feeling any such thing. The hard set of his face, the grim line of his mouth told her that he had meant the stark, harsh declaration.

Lie back and think of the money... Like sleeping with a horse... All her fears came rushing back in full force. She had disappointed him. Her inexperience had shown so that he hadn't even enjoyed being with her.

'And why is that?' she managed, her voice not sounding like her own.

'Virgins cling.' It was a flat, unyielding statement, his tone as dead as his eyes. It was obvious that the declaration came from past experience.

'And you don't want anyone clinging to you, I suppose?'

The brusque shake of his head was answer enough, but he underlined it with another adamant declaration.

'I told you—all that I stand up in and nothing more. No commitments, nothing long-term. Innocents don't want that. They have stars in their eyes—and dreams of Prince Charming and happy ever after.'

Not this virgin, Martha was tempted to fling back. She'd already had the stars knocked right out of her eyes once already today. She didn't need a second lesson.

But that was old Martha talking. The one who had got to twenty-three as a virgin because her life had not been her own until now. The one who had been sole carer for a dying mother for far longer than she cared to remember. The innocent, both in worldly and sexual terms, who really had been looking for a happy ever after when she had first met Gavin. And who had had stars in her eyes so bright that they had blinded her to the reality—that she was really only in love with the idea of being in love. She had vowed that she had left that Martha behind.

And—oh, dear heaven help her—she *wanted* this man. Even now, just sitting here, metres away from him, she could still feel the sexual pull that he exerted on her, the excitement he could create in her senses simply by existing. That long, lean body, with its broad shoulders and strong legs dominated the room, those stunning features, the carved cheekbones seeming even more dramatic in this light. His bronzed skin looked more golden, the burnished jet strands of his hair had dried soft and silky and appealingly disordered and his jaw was now shaded dark with the day's growth of beard, giving him a ruffianly, almost piratical look that was dangerously attractive.

The scent of his skin was clinging to her dress; the taste of his kisses was still in her mouth. If she slicked her tongue over her lips, she could waken that sensation all over again. It was the most exciting thing she had ever known—and she wanted more of it. But the unsmiling set of his sexy mouth and the dark green of his eyes warned her not to act on the attraction she felt.

'Maybe some women do,' she said carefully. 'But that's not what I want from you. Ships that pass in the night, remember? It was fun but…what are you doing?'

Isn't it obvious? The scathing look he turned on her demanded without words, but all the same he gave her an answer, the exaggerated patience of his tone making it sound savage and dangerous in spite of the fact that his voice hadn't been raised above the calmness of conversation.

'Getting dressed,' he stated flatly, snatching up his jeans from the floor where they had been discarded in the heat of their passion… Was it really only a few short minutes ago? Martha felt as if she had aged a lifetime since then. 'I need some air…'

'Fine.'

Virgins cling—do they indeed? Well, she was going to prove him wrong—at least where this virgin was concerned. She'd rather die than admit that it was tearing her in pieces to watch him pull on his clothes, fasten buttons, his belt, as if he needed to be armoured against her. She'd walked away from one man already today, she could do it again. Or, rather, she could let Carlos walk away from her. If he didn't want her then there was no way on earth that she was going to beg…

At least Carlos had wanted *her* that first time. And he *had* wanted her. Wanted her with a passion that couldn't be controlled and that had burned them up in the heat of the moment, impossible to deny and taking them both by storm. It seemed impossible that it could have burned itself out in the space of such a short time, when her own body still sizzled in the aftermath of the wild orgasm she had experienced. But if there was nothing left for Carlos but cold ashes then she was not going to humiliate herself by trying to keep him with her.

Spotting his tee shirt where she had flung it on the end of the bed, she bundled it up roughly and tossed it at him.

'You'll need this if you're going out. And this.' The battered leather jacket followed.

'*Gracias.*' It was a cynical drawl. But even as he shrugged the jacket on and zipped it up he turned to her again, eyes hooded, a new tightness around his beautiful mouth.

'Miss Jones,' he said, and if there was anything guaranteed to strike a new spark to light the fire of anger in Martha's heart then that was it.

Miss Jones. The Devil and Miss Jones. Two totally unreal people meeting and passing briefly—so briefly—in the night. He hadn't wanted to know her real name. He hadn't wanted to know the real *her*. It had been a moment out of time and now it was over. It might be hurting to know it had only lasted such a short time but the answer to dealing with anything that had come to an end was to break it off—sharp and clean. Over and done with.

'Still here?' she questioned coldly, making herself look him in the eye, forcing her own face into a controlled, unrevealing mask, totally blanked off from all emotion. 'I thought you were getting some air.'

And that brought the truth rushing into his face. The stark rejection of her presence in the room now that the passion had died between them. So it was true what her mother had always said—that once a man had had what he wanted, you didn't see him for dust. That was the way it had been with her father. He'd barely stuck around long enough to know that he'd got her mother pregnant.

'Goodbye, *Señor* Diablo,' she flung at him, deliberately turning away on the words.

Was he really going? She couldn't decide how she felt about it if he did. Was the emotion that tugged at her nerves one of disappointment, loss or just plain relief? Probably a mixture of all three and each one took its own turn at being uppermost. She only knew that if this was a challenge, an attempt to make her admit that she didn't want him to go, then she wasn't going to rise to it. Let him walk out, head off on his own in that so typically masculine way. She'd let him go and not say a word to hold him back.

So she clamped her lips tight shut and waited, nerves prickling all over her body in the silence that descended. She even tried not to listen so that she didn't hear him move, heard nothing at all until the slam of the door back into its frame announced loud and clear that he had walked out of it and that she was alone in the room.

So now what? Martha sank down onto the bed in a rush, letting her breath escape in a ragged sigh. Where did she go from here?

Virgins cling. The words that Carlos had tossed at her so savagely came back to circle in her thoughts, telling her there was really only one thing she could do.

If Carlos had known that she had never had a lover, then tonight would never have happened. He hadn't wanted to make love to a virgin—to take her innocence. He was convinced that she would cling, and she was determined not to do that. Well, there was one thing she could do to prove him wrong. She could go, get out of his life and leave him in peace.

Though she strongly suspected that peace probably wasn't the word that described Carlos Diablo's life right at this moment.

'Don't you have a job—a home—family who care

for you?' she had asked and his response had been dark, bitter laughter, that coldly flippant 'all I stand up in.'

Well, she couldn't help him with that. But she could at least show him that some people didn't try to force him into a situation he didn't want; they kept their word when they said they were asking for nothing more from him.

And she was asking for nothing. He'd said they were just ships that had passed in the night and the night, or at least the part of it they would spend together, was over now. She had no intention of being here when he got back. She could just imagine how he would greet the realisation if she had stayed. She had seen black disappointment settle over those stunning features once already tonight—and that was once too many. She couldn't bear to see it again.

Not giving herself time or a chance to change her mind, Martha pushed herself off the bed and began to collect up her belongings.

CHAPTER FIVE

Four months later

THE sound of the helicopter circling overhead had brought Martha to the door of the *estancia*, and now she watched as it swung down to the ground, blades whirling, making the trees sway, the dust spin upwards. Slowly and carefully it landed some distance from the main house. The calculated ease of the landing, the way that the big machine came down so smoothly that even the highly strung and immensely valuable polo ponies grazing in the fields not too far away were barely startled enough to fling up their heads was hugely impressive. Obviously the pilot had done this before. Many times.

'Your visitor has arrived, Javier,' Martha called back into the house, hearing the sound of the old man's wheelchair coming up behind her.

'I heard.'

Manoeuvring himself so that he could see out of the window, Javier Ortega watched as the rotating blades on top of the black and gold helicopter slowed and gradually stilled, nodding silently to himself as if to express some deep satisfaction.

'He will be staying for some time,' he said in his careful, rather stiff English. 'I assume you have the room ready?'

'Of course.' Martha smiled, remembering how he had wanted one particular room carefully prepared. 'Just as you asked. I dealt with it all myself.'

It was amazing, she reflected, just how easily she had settled into place here at the *estancia* named El Cielo. And so appropriately named, she acknowledged, looking round her at the wide expanse of fields that spread out from the big house, surrounded by stunning mountain views. The wild forest had been transformed into a natural park on one side where a huge lake lay calm and still in the silence of the evening. It was heaven on earth, and it had proved such a refuge to her when an unexpected twist of fate had taken her life and turned it upside down and inside out.

Her eyes were still on the helicopter, but her thoughts were back in the small, slightly shabby hotel room when she had shared one wild night—not even a night—of passion with the man who had called himself Carlos Diablo. That hadn't even been his real name, as she had discovered when realising that she couldn't leave the hotel, leave him, dressed only in the now dishevelled and torn wedding dress.

Carlos's travel bag had lain where he had dumped it earlier, the top still open so that she had been able to see the red cotton of a clean tee shirt poking out of it. As well as the tee shirt there had been some battered tracksuit trousers, too long and too wide, but with the help of the belt in the second pair of jeans she could just about manage to keep them up. Carlos really had been travelling light. The only other thing his bag had contained was a canvas travel wallet with passport and other documents. Curiosity overwhelming her, Martha had lifted it and pulled out the passport.

The photograph had obviously been taken some time before, and the Carlos in the picture looked younger, more approachable, easier in his own skin. There were lines etched on his face now that had not been there on this younger man. Whatever had happened to send him off on his travels had obviously changed him a lot in a very short space of time.

His name was different too, she realised with a shock. The name on this passport was Carlos Ortega, not Carlos Diablo. So he hadn't even wanted her to know who he really was—just as he had never wanted to know her proper name when she had tried to give it to him. He had truly meant for this to be a one-night thing and nothing else at all. So had he told her the truth about anything? This was an Argentinian passport, it seemed—and the address of next of kin...

Flicking through the pages, she found it. Javier Ortega. Carlos's grandfather, it seemed. And an address that meant nothing. But the name El Cielo was so evocative that she knew instantly it must be a spectacularly beautiful place. But Carlos had said that he had no family to leave behind, so had this Javier Ortega died?

It was all she'd had to go on though, and she could only be thankful that Javier Ortega's *estancia* had had such an evocative name, one that she'd instantly remembered when she'd needed to find a way to contact the Ortega family.

All she had been looking for had been an email or postal address, perhaps a phone number, just some way of being able to get in touch with the man who had passed through her life so briefly and dramatically just a few months before. A man she had never been able to forget, and who now she would always remember because of the effect of that night on the rest of her life. She had never ever expected that the beautiful sprawling cream and terracotta painted building would ever come to feel almost like a home to her as it had in the past weeks.

A home to her and to her unborn baby. Martha's hand slid under the floaty pink, white and turquoise tunic top she wore with stretchy leggings and touched the as yet barely visible swell where the child she had conceived on her one-night stand with Carlos lay peacefully, growing bigger every day. There had been a certain sort of poetic rightness about the fact that she had discovered that she was pregnant with Carlos's baby only a couple of weeks after she had arrived in his home country. Feeling restless and unsure of how to shape her future now that the married life she had been anticipating would never happen, she had decided to use some of the money she had won to travel, and, seeing as she couldn't get the meeting with Carlos Diablo out of her mind, visiting Argentina had seemed like an inevitable choice.

At first she had taken the lateness of her period as

the result of travel, the after effects of cancelling her wedding, but it had soon become clear that it was more than that. She had been shocked, bewildered, but secretly thrilled. She had been looking for a new direction for her life, and here was the perfect one. A new person to love, a new life to care for.

But she had known that Carlos too had a right to know about the baby—his child. She knew what it was like to grow up without a father and it was not what she wanted for her baby. Just the thought of confronting him with the fact made her skin feel cold, her heart clench in apprehension. She had little doubt that he would want nothing to do with the baby—*No commitments, nothing long-term*—the memory of his voice was so clear that it was almost as if he were speaking right in her ear. But he had the right to know that he was going to be a father at least and that meant she had to find a way of telling him.

'Is there just the pilot?' she asked now, suddenly wondering if perhaps the man who had flown the helicopter had been doing so to deliver someone else, one of Javier's hugely wealthy friends, to El Cielo.

'Just him,' the old man confirmed. 'He flies his own 'copter. Damn this chair—I could have gone down to meet him.'

'He'll be here soon enough,' Martha reassured him, well used to the old man's frustration at being confined to the wheelchair.

Events had conspired against her when Javier Ortega, who had invited her to El Cielo for a short stay while he tried to track down his missing grandson, had been taken ill on the day after she had arrived. A stroke had put him in hospital and she hadn't been able to leave him without care or company when he had come home again, now confined to the chair. So she had stayed, acting as the old man's carer, and waiting for the news that Javier had managed to get in touch with Carlos, that he had an address or a phone number.

Shading her eyes against the setting sun, Martha watched as the rotating blades finally stilled and a door in the helicopter opened, a dark, shadowed figure getting out. A dark, shadowed, masculine shape. A tall, powerfully built man who jumped lithely to the ground before turning to stare towards the house. And something in the movement tugged at Martha's thoughts, stirring memories she had believed were carefully buried. He was too far away to see clearly but a cold hand seemed to reach out and twist her nerves tight as she fought for control.

'I'll go and check on the food...' she began hastily, knowing that it was just a memory that had caught on something raw and vulnerable deep inside her, and it was not to be trusted in any way.

In the huge modern kitchen, she busied herself with checking on the beef in the oven, the vegetables prepared and waiting to be cooked. There was red wine 'breathing', the dessert in the fridge. Nothing needed doing and she knew she had only hurried in here to distract herself from the restless, uncomfortable feeling that just the sight of a tall, dark-haired man, seen from a distance, had sparked off in her. It was stupid, it was crazy, it was...

'My…Javier said that I should come and tell you to stop hiding yourself away in here…'

The voice from the kitchen door behind her had her freezing into the stillness of total, blind panic. Sensations like the burn of ice stung their way over her skin, making her shiver in uncontrolled response as just those few words stripped away the intervening months and dragged her right back to the day of her aborted wedding and a small, slightly shabby hotel bedroom where her life had changed for ever.

She had heard that voice in her thoughts, so many times since then. Heard it in her dreams and woken, shaking, in a tangle of bedclothes and sweat, with moisture on her cheeks that she tried to pretend had nothing to do with tears. It had echoed through her imagination but she had never believed that she would ever hear it again in reality.

Javier had told her that he would track down Carlos if he possibly could. His grandson had left no forwarding address but if he could be found then he'd make it happen. It had only taken a few days for her to warm to the brusque and obviously lonely old man whose pride would not let him admit that he needed anyone. While he had been in hospital she had visited him, taken him the things he needed and when he had come home he had asked her to stay. With memories of the way she had once helped her ailing mother still fresh in her head, she had soon slipped into the role of his carer and had been glad to stay as long as he wanted her.

When the thought that perhaps she was also staying so that she could be close to Carlos in a way, living in this place that had once been home to him, slid into her mind, she pushed it away impatiently. She needed to tell Carlos that she had conceived his child during their one night together, it was the only just and fair thing to do, but after that she was going to be fine, no matter what he decided to do about the baby. She had no illusions, no foolish dreams that he might ever want to have any sort of relationship with her or, probably, with his child. But she wouldn't need him. She had more than enough money to care for herself and this little one for the rest of their lives. If Carlos wanted nothing to do with the baby then that would be his loss.

But it was one thing to have resolved to tell Carlos by phone or letter—quite another now to discover that the 'visitor' Javier had told her was arriving today was in fact Carlos himself.

'Did you hear what I said?' Carlos's voice had a sharp edge to it but obviously he hadn't yet realised who she was. Why should he when the last time he had seen her had been on a dark, rainy night in England and as far as he knew she had never even known his real name?

And he had never wanted to know hers. That memory stabbed at her cruelly so that she had to clamp her lips tight closed to hold back the sudden cry of distress that almost escaped her as she fought for the control she needed.

'*Señorita…*' It was a definite note of warning now and she could hear the way that his patience was fraying at the edges in the emphasis he put on it.

'I heard…'

The words seemed to come from lips that were made

of wood, they were so stiff and tight. But even as she said them she was nerving herself to turn round and face him. The nasty little struggle she was having with herself put an impetus into the movement that swung her round abruptly and with much more force than she had ever anticipated so that she almost bumped into the tall, dark man behind her. She hadn't expected him to be so close. She hadn't been aware of the way that he had come up behind her on silent feet, so that they were almost touching, the warmth of his hard body reaching out to surround her, the scent of his skin rushing into her nostrils with the sudden startled gasp of reaction that she drew in.

She wasn't yet ready to see him, see that stunning, harshly carved face, those deep, deep green eyes that would surely be burning with anger and rejection at the sight of her. It was bad enough keeping her gaze focused on the expanse of broad chest in front of her, the immaculate white shirt and—dear heaven, he was actually wearing that same battered leather jacket that had featured so vividly in the dreams that had haunted her nights since she had last seen him! She could still remember just how it had felt to have that soft worn leather fold around her, the lining warm from his body and retaining the scent of his skin so that it was like being enclosed in the arms of the man himself.

'I heard you,' she managed shakily, not daring to lift her eyes to his to see the shock that must show in his face. But she knew the moment he recognised her, saw it in the change of his stance, the way his breathing snagged, caught, then started again with a rough and obviously furious new rhythm.

'You! What the hell are you doing here?' he demanded, and if she had ever been under any illusion that he might actually want to see her again then that foolish dream flew right out of the window with each coldly brutal and icily enunciated syllable he spoke.

'I...Your grandfather invited me...'

It was as if she'd pressed her finger on some raw spot on his skin so that he reacted sharply, eyes narrowing, jaw tightening, and she saw the way that his mouth compressed as if he was holding back whatever it had been his first impulse to say.

'I'll just bet he did,' Carlos scorned. 'He always had an eye for a pretty face so that women find him easy to wrap around their little fingers. But how the hell did you find out about El Cielo?'

'It's in your passport...'

'Ah yes, of course, my passport.' Carlos's tone thickened with contempt. 'You went through my things—stole a few items too, as I remember.'

'Not stole!' Martha protested sharply. The tee shirt and the tracksuit trousers were upstairs in her bedroom, carefully washed and pressed with an attention to detail that was at odds with their elderly, battered condition.

'Not stole,' Carlos echoed caustically, nodding blackly cynical agreement. 'I suppose that you always intended to give them back to me.'

He was implying something more than simply that she would return his clothes to him, but, still off balance because of the shock of his arrival, Martha couldn't work out just what.

'I did! I've never stolen anything from anyone and…'

'And that is why you're here, of course—you travelled all this way simply to return my clothes.' Black cynicism roughened his voice. 'And that's also why you went through my belongings—checked out my passport.'

'I could hardly have walked out of there in my wedding dress!' Martha protested. She knew that looking at his passport was the thing he really objected to and under normal circumstances she would be in total agreement with him. But these weren't exactly normal circumstances. 'And as to checking out your passport—well, you had never actually told me your real name.'

'And this bothered you because… *Miss Jones*?'

The savage bite of acid on the name she had given him made her flinch away inside. She knew exactly what that pointed remark meant.

'All right, so neither did I!' she flung at him. 'I didn't give you my name because…'

Because you didn't want it, memory reminded her. *Because you said we were just two ships that passed in the night and nothing more.*

And it was frightening to realise that the memory hurt. Because she didn't want to feel this way about it, not when he so obviously didn't feel anything like the same. She knew now that she had wanted him to need to know more about her. To feel more about her than just the blazing passion that had driven him that night. He clearly hadn't spared her a thought in the time they had been apart. From the look on his face now he didn't want to be confronted by her at all, and had only the darkest suspicions about why she was here. While she had never been able to get him out of her thoughts from the moment she had first met him. And he had haunted her dreams on so many disturbed nights since she had walked away from him.

'Because we didn't have that sort of a relationship. "'I'm not looking for forever,'" he tossed at her. "All I care about is now.'"

He'd thought she meant it, Carlos remembered. He'd also thought that it had suited him just fine on that cold wet April day just four months before. They had both been lost, drifting souls, wandering in a world that had suddenly changed so dramatically that they had completely lost their bearings. They hadn't had anything to give to each other but the closeness of their bodies, that incandescent spiralling desire that had gripped them both, driving him half out of his mind with wanting. So much so that he had forgotten every trace of common sense, every rule by which he lived.

He had shocked himself by his crazy behaviour, the irresponsibility of his loss of control. He hadn't behaved like that since he had been a horny teenager at the mercy of his hormones and he didn't recognise himself in the man he had become. Particularly when he'd seen how the condom they had used had not really protected them, tearing badly in the final mad consummation. The realisation of his own stupidity had driven him out of that room, away from its claustrophobic confines for a brief space of time, needing to drag some cold air into his burning lungs and hope to clear his head. Then he might be able to talk to her with some degree of control and sanity when he got back.

He had meant to talk to her. He'd wanted to talk to her, to try to make sense of the hot-wired connection they had made so fiercely and so fast—physically at least. He had wanted to know more about her. He had even considered that, lost and obviously adrift as she was, facing up to the way that her future had been turned inside out just as his had, she might actually be able to understand something of the way that his life had blown apart. He had even found that he was contemplating spending an evening no longer alone as he had been for a couple of weeks now with a sort of anticipation, if not quite pleasure. He had liked the way that as Miss Jones and Carlos Diablo they were meeting completely fresh, with no preconceptions, no past knowledge about each other. She had shown no sign of recognising him, knew nothing of his own wealth, of the inheritance of the Ortega fortune he was supposed to be heir to, the huge income that his time as a champion polo player, the horses he had bred with an instinctive eye for pedigree and bloodlines, had brought him. And after years of meeting women with money signs in their eyes when they looked at him, that had been such an intense relief.

And if he didn't know anything more about her than her name, and the second thoughts she had had about her planned wedding, then he had actually been looking forward to finding out. Perhaps it was time to rethink the personal rule he had had about never making love to virgins—perhaps that had become as irrelevant to his new way of life as the name and inheritance he had once thought was his. And certainly he had found that the prospect of a night—maybe more—spent in Miss Jones's warm, silken arms, enjoying the pleasures of her sexy, voluptuous body, made the blood pulse in his veins, his feet turning instinctively back towards the hotel he had just left.

But when he had returned to the room she had gone. The bedroom had been empty; the only indication that she had ever been there at all the bundle of once-white silk. The wedding dress, dumped in the corner.

And the money. The bundle of notes, carefully weighted down with the room service menu. Something flared at the memory. The same mixture of anger, confusion and disbelief that he had felt on the night when he had first seen the cash she had left behind, and he was no nearer unravelling the knot of feeling than he had been then.

'You left me money!'

She actually looked surprised; stunned was more like it. Those big grey eyes looked up into his as if she couldn't believe what he had said.

'Of course I did.'

'And why was that?'

He knew it was the memory of how he had felt then that was kicking at him. He hadn't been able to believe that she had just turned and run out on him. Gone, without a word; without a hint of anything. She had disappeared from his life as quickly and as mysteriously as she had come into it. And he had had no way of finding out who she was or where she had gone.

He'd told himself that that was what he wanted. But now that he'd got exactly that, the most disturbing sense of loss had plagued him.

'What did you think it was?'

'Payment for services rendered?'

It was meant to be an attempt at dark humour but the buzzing confusion as to just what he actually felt made sure that it missed the target by a mile. Recalling how he had once wanted to see her again made the fact that she had tracked him down to El Cielo now twist in his guts. It meant that she had to have investigated the Carlos Ortega he had kept hidden—which put a very different slant on this, making it so much more than just a reunion.

'What? Oh, don't be ridiculous! I thought you might need the money—to pay for the hotel—but that was a lie too, wasn't it?'

He was definitely wary now. The loss of 'Miss Jones' and Carlos Diablo had a sting that rocked his sense of balance. She had gone through his belongings, found his passport, which would have told her where he had once lived—when he had believed that Javier Ortega was truly his grandfather. It would only have taken a name inserted into an Internet search engine, a couple of clicks to find out more. Now she had turned up here like this, inveigling her way into Javier's life. Just what was it she was after?

And she was accusing *him* of lying.

'How did I lie to you?'

It would help if the physical impact of her nearness didn't hit home quite so much. She had cut her hair since he had last seen her and the new, slightly shorter style exposed the soft, vulnerable curve of her neck. Her skin had acquired a light golden tan after some time in the sunshine of Argentina and as a result her soft grey eyes looked huge and stunning with long lush lashes framing their pale colour. The vivid colours of her flowing top were bright and warm, a contrast to the all-white look of her wedding gown. She looked to have put on a little weight, and he liked the extra swell of her breasts under the delicate cotton, the curve to her hips in the clinging leggings. And there was that sensual perfume that had been his downfall before and now swirled around his senses like pure temptation, dangerously intoxicating.

She looked different. Just what had happened to her in the four months since that night in the hotel? It wasn't just the touch of the sun that had put that colour in her face. Something—or someone—had put that bloom in her cheeks. Another man? Was that what had happened to her? Rejection jagged through him at just the thought.

'You claimed that you were penniless… Wine and horses,' she added now. 'You neglected to mention the stud farm, the vineyards. "All that I stand up in…"'

'That was all that I had with me at the time. Not that you gave me any more details about yourself, did you, my dear Miss…?'

He caught himself up sharply, realising that something that might have worked for the moments out of time of a crazy, wild one-night stand could not possibly be continued into the reality of everyday life. It was the first thing he would have asked if she had been waiting when he'd got back to the hotel room.

'What the hell is your name? I can't just keep on calling you Miss Jones.'

'Why not?' she enquired sardonically. 'I reckon it will do as well as "Carlos Diablo"—if I hadn't seen your passport, I would never have known who you really are. Which was what you wanted in the first place, wasn't it?'

'You didn't ask for proof of identity.'

'I was in a desperate situation and you knew it. So you gave me some made-up name...'

'Not made-up. Diablo is my middle name.'

It was as much his real name as Carlos Ortega. He might have grown up with that proud surname all his life, but when he had learned that his father had never been the man he had believed him to be then he had lost both his name and his family history and with it any real knowledge of his identity. Javier Ortega, the man he had once believed to be his grandfather, had thrown him out, turned his back on him and walked away, which was what made it so incredible that the stubborn old man had ever summoned him back here again.

But now that he had realised that Miss Jones was here, it put a very different slant on things. Was she somehow involved in Javier's change of mind?

'It certainly wasn't your real name. But I suppose it was good enough when all you planned to do was to seduce me and walk out on me.'

'You did your share of the seducing. You're not going

to claim that you weren't more than willing. And as I recall you did the walking out too.'

'Well, of course. You surely didn't expect me to be sitting in that room just waiting for you?'

'As a matter of fact I did.'

'I don't see why.' She shrugged off his response. 'You weren't looking for commitment and neither was I. What we had together was fine—for one night. No one owes the other anything after that.'

'Not even a name?'

She looked as if she would still like to hold out on that but at that moment Carlos heard the swish of wheel tyres on the polished wood floor and knew that Javier was coming up behind him. To see the old man in that chair had been a shock on his arrival. He'd known that Javier had been ill, because he'd kept tabs on just how he was doing, but he'd had no idea that this was the lingering effect of that.

'Marta?' The old man sounded crabby and impatient. 'Are we ever going to eat or do you plan on spending all evening in the kitchen?'

'It's almost ready,' she assured him, her tone soothing, and she turned a smile in his direction that obviously smoothed some of the ruffled feathers and even, Carlos was stunned to see, brought something of an answering light into the old man's watery eyes. 'Why don't you take Carlos back to the dining room and I'll be with you in just a few minutes? You could pour him a drink,' she added to Carlos.

And to emphasise the way that she wanted to put

a distance between them she took a careful couple of steps backwards, widening the gap between them.

'I will,' Carlos told her, frankly surprised at the way that the stubborn and cantankerous Javier had allowed himself to be pacified and was now manoeuvring his chair in a circle to turn around and head out of the room again. Something twisted sharply deep inside at the realisation of how long it had been since he'd seen an expression like that on Javier's face. 'Marta...?'

'It's Martha actually,' she told him crisply, reaching for a pair of oven gloves ready to take the meat out of the oven. 'But Javier always pronounces it that way.'

'Martha Jones. That is, always assuming that the Jones part is the truth.'

'Of course it is. I only gave you part of my name—but it was all the truth. I wasn't the one who was lying.'

'I told no lies,' Carlos shot back.

She was getting under his skin now, and that wasn't just from the irritation at being called a liar. The movement she had made towards the oven had made her breasts sway softly in a way that had his body responding in the most primitively basic masculine reaction, the rush of blood that hardened him making him shift uncomfortably. And the heat from the oven brought out the scent of her body even more so that he felt as if he was becoming heavily intoxicated as if inhaling some potent and mind-altering drug.

'Diablo—Ortega?' she mocked. 'One of those isn't the truth.'

'It's complicated.'

Complicated and personal. So personal that he didn't

want to share it with her. At least not now. Not when he
had no idea why she was here. The memory of the way
that he had actually felt, that he might have shared it
with her—with 'Miss Jones'—on that night came back
to haunt him and he felt a rush of thankfulness that he
had been spared the foolishness of opening up to someone he couldn't have ever really trusted.

At that moment Javier, who had been heading off
down the corridor to the huge dining room that stood
open to the evening sun, suddenly came to a halt and
looked round impatiently.

'Are you coming to get this drink or not?' he demanded.

'Coming, Ab—' Carlos responded, hastily biting
back the word *abuelo*—grandfather—that had come
automatically to his tongue but that he had no right to
use any more. 'Coming,' he finished more curtly.

He would bide his time and wait and watch things,
he told himself as he followed the old man out of the
kitchen. Wait and see just why he had been summoned
here. A sense of bitter disappointment stabbed at him
as he remembered how he had felt when Javier's phone
call had come through. The unexpected summons back
to El Cielo had stirred hopes of reconciliation, being, if
not welcomed, then at least allowed back into the house
that had once been his family home. Back into the world
that was all the family he had ever known. He hadn't
known quite what he had been expecting but it wasn't
this.

For a moment he glanced back and saw where Miss
Jones—Martha—was busying herself in the kitchen.

She looked so much at home, so comfortably settled in a way that he no longer felt, that it turned a knife in his heart just to see it. He would once have been the one cooking steaks, pouring wine for a casual end-of-the-day meal with Javier. Now it seemed his place had been usurped—and by the woman he had had a one-night stand with just a few months before.

Just what the hell was she doing here?

The worrying thing was that she wouldn't be here if it weren't for him. If she hadn't found out about his real name, his connection to the vast Ortega fortune. So had that brought little Miss Jones, Miss 'all I stand up in' running to Argentina like the gold-digger it seemed she was, looking for the man she believed was the heir to that estate? *Querido Dios*, after the way that his mother had betrayed both her husband and Javier, was it possible that now he had brought the old man to the attention of another predatory woman?

The fury and disgust at himself that flooded him took him back once again to the reason why he had had to get out of that hotel bedroom when he had realised that his lack of control had led him to break one of his most personal rules. And that now he would have to deal with the fallout from that.

Reaching for a bottle of wine, he set himself to opening it, wrenching out the cork with rather more force than was actually necessary. Martha had had a real problem meeting his eyes and she had been as edgy as a cat on a hot roof. She was hiding something, that much was obvious, and he was determined to discover just what her secret was.

And when he did, then he would know exactly how to deal with her.

CHAPTER SIX

ONE of the greatest pleasures of Martha's stay on the *estancia* El Cielo had always been the luxury of being able to swim in the outdoor pool, particularly while Javier was still asleep and before he needed her. Since the morning sickness that had plagued her at first had eased off, she had enjoyed having the place to herself and being able to indulge in some gentle exercise before the heat of the day made her feel limp and out of sorts.

But not this morning. After an uncomfortable and tense evening meal where her appetite had totally deserted her and she had only been able to pick at her food, she had endured an unrefreshing, restless night. Anxiety and apprehension had kept her tossing and turning, finding it impossible to drift off into anything more than an uneasy doze. So she had been awake even earlier than usual this morning and, giving up on trying to rest, had slipped from her room at the back of the house, creeping down the staircase to the pool. The cool of the water was like balm to her overheated and sensitised skin and the smooth regular movement soothed her more than her attempts at sleep had ever done.

Today was going to have to be the day, she admitted

to herself as she swam carefully, almost silently, from one end of the pool to another. No matter what happened, she couldn't endure another night like the last one. She had to tell Carlos why she was here, get that off her chest, and then she could look to the future, make plans to become a mother and to care for her child.

Slipping a hand under the water, she spread it against the barely visible swell of her womb under the clinging dark blue swimming costume, not daring to think of just how Carlos might react when she told him about the baby. It had been bad enough facing him so unexpectedly yesterday.

She could only imagine that Javier had thought he was doing the right thing, inviting Carlos here like this. He had known she was pregnant from early on. One very hot day she had fainted and Javier had insisted on calling the doctor. But he had only promised to find an address or a phone number for her, not force her to confront the father of her child. At least he had kept to his promise not to tell him about the baby, but to wait until she did that herself. But several times last night she could see that he was itching to bring everything out into the open and only several desperate glances when Carlos wasn't looking had stopped him just in time.

'Is the water nice?'

The question came out of the blue, it seemed, reaching her just as she came to the end of the pool and brought her feet to the ground, ready to get out.

'What?'

Her shocked gasp brought a rush of water into her

eyes and she had to pause, swiping at her face until her vision cleared and she could see clearly.

But she knew who it was, of course. The deep dark tones of that smooth, sexy voice with its gorgeous accent were etched into her memory, telling her that the subject of her thoughts, Carlos himself, was standing on the side of the pool, feet placed firmly wide apart on the pale blue and white tiles. He had obviously just got out of bed, not even troubling to run a comb through the thick black hair that was ruffled into disorder that softened it from its normal ruthlessly controlled neatness. And that unexpected disarray was combined with a night's growth of beard that darkened his jaw giving him a piratical look that was dangerously appealing. His strong frame was etched against the rising sun, a dark commanding force that seemed ominous and threatening for all that his question had been in a mild, seemingly conversational tone.

'It's lovely,' she managed, as she watched him warily. He had clearly come out for an early morning swim just like her and navy swimming shorts hugged his lean hips and powerful legs, curving over the bulge of his masculinity in a way that made her mouth dry uncomfortably.

'I'm sure it is,' Carlos murmured, but this time there was definitely something in his voice that made it plain that he was not just making an innocuous remark. There was a dangerous, dark undertone to the word that made her shiver.

'Just what is that supposed to mean?' she snapped,

regretting it immediately. It was far better to play this carefully and not risk antagonising him.

But the look he turned on her was one of mild indifference, almost surprise at her reaction.

'Merely that living here in luxury at El Cielo—must seem like a delight to you after what you're used to.'

'You don't know what I'm used to...'

'But you told me your father had walked out on you—and that you'd spent the last years nursing your mother. That can't have been easy. Money must have been tight.'

Amazed that he had even remembered the brief conversation they had had on the moors, Martha could only duck her head in a brusque, brief nod, suddenly feeling overawed and shockingly vulnerable by the way his tall figure towered over her, the black shadow he cast blocking out the sun.

'It was.'

'And now?'

'I'm—managing.'

'But there would have been the wedding to pay for— even if it never took place.'

That brought her head up in a rush, her eyes widening in surprise; surprise that he would even care.

'There was that. But I'd sold the flat Mum and I lived in.'

It was part of the truth. And he accepted it without question. But after all that had happened she was still reluctant to open up about everything—including the money she had won. Money that had made clearing up the mess after her wedding so much easier. The truth was that she'd simply written a huge cheque for her wedding planner and left the woman to deal with everything. She'd never wanted to see the Hall, her now thankfully very ex-fiancé, or the bridesmaid who had betrayed her ever again.

'We were supposed to be buying a house together.' Or, rather, she had been expected to buy that house. 'So I had no ties. And I wanted to get away.'

'Was there much fallout from the wedding that never was?'

'Much less than I'd anticipated. It seemed that several people already knew that Gavin was playing away and so very few were really surprised that I backed out almost at the altar.'

It felt as if she were talking about events that had happened to someone else, in a time long ago, so distant that it was barely even a memory to her. While the time she had spent with this man, those few short hours, was etched into her memory like vivid scenes from a stunning film, played over and over again and crowding into her thoughts at night to prevent her from sleeping.

'No regrets?'

And that at least was easy to answer. Lifting her head, she looked him straight in the eye, her expression totally sure, totally confident.

'None whatsoever. It was the best decision I ever made.'

She caught hold of the edges of the metal ladder to climb out of the pool, then stopped abruptly, awareness sneaking over her skin like a cold breeze. The signs of her pregnancy were only slight at the moment, but her wet swimming costume would cling far too tightly, revealing every small detail of the curve to her belly, the way her breasts had swollen. She might have come here to tell Carlos about the baby but the last thing she wanted to do was to emerge from the water in all the glory of her changing body. She might as well throw out her arms, blowing a fake fanfare, and announce, *Ta dah! Guess what's happened to me!*

Her stomach twisted at just the thought and she hastily dipped back under the water again, gesturing with a wave of her arm towards where her towel lay draped across a wooden sun lounger a few metres away.

'Can you pass me that—please?' She made herself add the last word, expecting, and getting, the twist of his mouth in response to her request.

'A bit late for modesty, isn't it, *querida*? After all, that night we spent together meant that I have seen much more of you than you will be revealing now.'

But all the same he reached for the towel, tossed it in her direction so that she only just caught it before it landed right in the water. It was something of a struggle to climb up the ladder and out into the sunlight, wrap the towel around her to conceal her burgeoning shape and still keep some dignity. And it wasn't helped by the memory of the way he had left her, not naked as his words implied, but with her ruined wedding dress ripped and crumpled, pulled up around her waist and down to expose her breasts. She had not only lost her virginity that night, she'd lost her pride and something of her soul when he'd rejected her and walked out. It had hurt so much more than Gavin's betrayal. The bitter memory of the way that she'd thought she'd found herself—the new Martha Jones—made bile rise in her throat and she knotted the towel so tightly around herself that it dug into her breasts and pinched her skin where it was fastened.

'We had sex,' she declared, stalking towards him, her head held high. 'That was all. We didn't even spend the night together.'

'And whose choice was that?' Carlos returned sardonically, folding strong arms together over his broad chest. The question brought Martha to an abrupt halt when she had hoped to march straight past him, not even looking in his direction.

'You're not telling me you wanted me to stay.'

'I certainly never anticipated that you would turn round and run out as soon as my back was turned.'

'And why is that? Do all your conquests just wait around when you've walked out on them after declaring that sleeping with them was a terrible mistake, something you wish had never happened? I'm sorry if I didn't come up to the standard you expected. But it was my first time!'

That hit home, she realised, a sense of triumph warring with a searing misery as she saw the way he reacted to her outburst. He winced—he actually winced and she saw with a bitter sense of satisfaction the way that his long body recoiled in the face of her attack.

'That was never what I meant,' he came back swiftly. 'You were wonderful—beautiful. How could I ever regret taking you to my bed? But it shouldn't have happened like that. Simply because it was your first time.'

'And when you found that out it was you who wanted me gone—you never wanted to see me again.'

'I sure as hell didn't expect to find that you'd moved in with my grandfather.'

'As in "made a move on…"?' Martha snapped back. 'Well, for your information, *Señor* Ortega—or Diablo—your grandfather gave me a job. I'm here as his carer, seeing as there was no one else.'

She'd scored another hit with that remark. This time Carlos's face twisted in a dark, savage scowl, one that made her take a hasty couple of steps back and away from him before she caught hold of herself and forced herself to stay where she was and confront him.

'Is that meant to imply that I have neglected him?' he snarled. 'That I should have been here to do the job instead?'

'If the cap fits,' Martha parried defiantly, though a new uncertainty crept into her voice.

There had been a distinct change in his expression at her comment, a darkening of those deep green eyes but in something that was very far from anger. Something she couldn't begin to understand, but instinct told her that she had trampled in where others might fear to tread and she had very definitely flung open a whole new Pandora's box of trouble.

'I would have been here if he'd let me!' Carlos flung at her now. 'If he'd told me how unwell he's been—how weak he'd become. Instead I had to wait until he summoned me here—and when I saw him in that chair…'

He didn't have to express his shock or the way he felt about it. It was there in the loss of colour in his face, the shake he couldn't quite iron out of his voice.

'You didn't know about that?'

'If I had, do you think I would have left him here alone?' There was a raw edge to his voice that scraped on her already exposed nerves.

'No,' Martha admitted. 'No, I know that you wouldn't. I saw the way you were with him last night.'

He had been alert to every move, every sound the old man made, always ready to pour a glass of wine or water, to pass food or snatch up the napkin that had fallen to the floor. And when Javier had announced that he was tired, Carlos had got to his feet and made sure that the way to his room was free, open for easy movement of the wheelchair. He hadn't offered to push it, instinctively understanding that that would be more than Javier's pride could accept. But he had been there standing by, close, in case he was needed.

'You never took your eyes off him. But you didn't have to wait till he "summoned" you—he is your grandfather.'

'But that's just the point, my dear *señorita*,' Carlos drawled, switching on the sort of cold-eyed smile that she thought was meant to show how little he cared but in fact ended up revealing exactly the opposite. 'The truth is that he is not.'

That had stopped her in her tracks, Carlos thought on a twist of something that was strangely close to regret. Seeing the way that those soft grey eyes widened in an expression of stunned surprise, he had to wonder just what was going through her mind. Was she really as confused as she appeared, or had she just seen the careful plan of cashing in on their past meeting disappearing as reality dawned?

Well, welcome to the club, he added cynically. Not that Javier's money mattered a damn. He had more than enough wealth of his own so that being the old man's grandson didn't matter for that type of legacy. It was the other sort of inheritance that mattered. The one of blood, of family, of belonging. The inheritance that had been taken from him with one stroke of a swab in his mouth, a laboratory test and a result that showed he was no relative of Javier Ortega, had no right at all to the proud Ortega name. He had lost his family, his birthright, his ancestry in the space of a couple of lonely heartbeats and everything he had ever believed himself to be, to belong to, had been taken away from him along with his identity, even his name.

'He's…not?' she managed, confusion clouding those beautiful eyes.

He could almost believe that she understood something of what he was feeling, but how could that be the case if it was him, Javier's grandson, that she had come to find? No, it had to be disappointment—because it was disappointment, not the imagined sympathy, that had almost made a fool out of him—that showed in her shocked gaze, the way that her teeth worried at the soft fullness of her lower lip.

A disappointment that seemed to be echoed in his own soul as once again he looked back at the Miss Jones who had known nothing of the truth about him, but had seen him simply as the man she had met on the moors.

'He's no relation of mine at all,' he stated flatly. 'I always thought he was. At least that was the way I was brought up, but about nine months ago, feeling his age I suppose, Javier decided to rewrite his will. He had a new lawyer, one who wanted everything done by the book, and he was the one who put the idea that *Abuelo* needed proof I was actually his grandson into his head.'

'But what about your parents?'

'The man I thought was my father—Javier's only son—was killed in a flying accident years ago when I was nine. He and my mother had been separated for some time before that but she had left me to live here at El Cielo because she wanted it that way. And because she wanted me to get close to the old man so that he would make me his heir.'

When—and why—had she taken a couple of steps to come closer? This close she was too much of a physical distraction, diverting his thoughts from the control he wanted to impose over them. The simple navy-blue one-piece swimming costume she wore contrasted sharply with the softly tanned skin he could see on display, still sheened with the water from the pool. From breast to hip the shape of her body was disguised by the bulky white towel, but he could still see the lean length of her legs, the slender thighs and calves, the narrow, arched feet with pink painted toenails that he had last seen covered in mud and dirt.

With her hair just beginning to dry softly in the warmth of the early morning she reminded him of the woman he had carried into the hotel on a cold wet night, and the memory gave him such a kick of lust that he was grateful for the fact he carried his own towel, holding the folds in front of himself to hide his body's instinctive response to her nearness. The sun must be going to his head too. He had never opened up to anyone about this family situation since it had all blown up in his face.

'So did they do a test?'

She was worrying at her bottom lip again, digging sharp white teeth in so that he wanted to reach out and lay a finger along her mouth, to make her stop. But he knew that if he did that it wouldn't end there. She was so close now that the scent of her body was winding its way around his senses, making the blood pound in his veins so that he was sure she must almost hear his heart thudding or see the pulse in his exposed neck. It wasn't the rising sun that was making his skin burn, his mouth dry.

'Yeah. DNA.' The fight he was having against his own responses made the reply rough and curt.

'And the result?'

'What do you think?' He didn't feel great about the way that she flinched back from the glare he shot her, but the memory of the way the news had been delivered to him had pushed him past being in full control of how he expressed himself. 'I told you—Javier Ortega is not my grandfather.'

Did she know what it did to him when she turned that look on him, the sympathy and understanding having an effect like having the cells of his skin brushed the wrong way so that they lifted and scraped uncomfortably, making him grit his teeth against the sensation? He wished he'd never started this, now. How had it happened that his plan of warning her off from making a play for Javier turned into the sort of self-exposure that he had never shared with anyone else before, not even his best friend?

'Your father was not your biological parent? And your mother had lied. That must have hurt.'

'Not as much as knowing that Javier only wanted me in his life if his blood ran through my veins.'

He'd really shocked her now. He could see it in the way that her head went back, those stunning grey eyes opening even wider in reaction. There was a certain grim satisfaction in seeing that this little detail, the one that had really stuck a knife in and twisted it, affected her almost as strongly as it had him.

'But that's horrible. And I do know something of how that feels. My father never wanted me or he'd have tried to make contact, even after he left my mother. But at least I always knew that my mother loved me—I never doubted that. I can't believe that Javier could turn from you like that.'

'I reckon he thought he owed it to his son.' He'd had time to think about this, to realise something of what had been behind Javier's behaviour. 'You had a father who didn't want you. I had one who loved me—but who'd been betrayed by his wife. So when Javier found out, he couldn't bear to have me around as the evidence of that betrayal of his beloved son. He must also have been furious at the way my mother had used him—leaving me in his care. So he told me to get out.'

'And you just took off—broke off all contact? You said you had no family in Argentina.'

'I don't—he disinherited me.'

'So the money is what mattered?'

'No way!' The strength of his rejection could leave her in no doubt he was telling the truth.

'Then what was it? The name?'

'A damn name doesn't matter! It's belonging that does!'

The ferocity in his tone made her wince—but she knew she was feeling *for* him, not because of the savagery he had turned on her.

'We all have a need to know where we belong. My mother and I never had much, but we had each other. You thought you belonged here—but he took that away from you. But you're here now.' He could see that it was meant to reassure but it had precisely the opposite effect.

'He asked,' he tossed at her, praying she wouldn't take it any further.

But she did.

'He asked—and you came. What do you think that reveals about the way you both feel? He wouldn't have asked you to come if—'

And that was too much. 'No, *belleza*, you have it completely wrong. He didn't ask me because he wanted me here—he only asked me to come because of you.'

And she couldn't deny that, he could see it in her eyes, in the sudden stillness of her glorious body.

'Oh, no...'

She shook her head almost violently, making the

golden strands fly out around her head, and one of them caught on the early morning stubble he hadn't troubled to get rid of before coming down to the pool. But then he hadn't expected to see anyone here. He still felt the burn of the shock of seeing her sleek, shapely body in the pool, smooth arms slicing through water, long, tanned legs kicking to propel her forward.

'I'm, sorry—'

Impulsively she moved forward to free her hair, her hand coming up in the same moment as his so that their fingers met, connected, froze. Electricity seemed to sizzle between them, scorching the skin. But at the same time they couldn't snatch away, break the contact. The combination of soft damp hair, fine warm skin, the rasp of stubble held him transfixed, staring down into her wide, dazed eyes.

From this angle he had a perfect view of her long, slender neck, the smooth curves of her shoulders. The white towel might be knotted tightly around her torso but it didn't conceal the swell of her breasts. If anything it emphasised the shadowed valley between them where they disappeared under the tight material. If he bent his head just so slightly then their mouths would meet, their lips coming into the contact he hungered for. He would taste her sweetness, feel the moist warmth of her lips, her tongue. He wanted it—he wanted her— but the bite of suspicion put a fierce check on the burn of need. She had followed him here, made herself at home with Javier. Yes, Javier had given her a job and any fool could see that she was good at caring for the stubborn old man, she had just the right touch with him, but there had to be more to it than that. No one travelled thousands of miles, across another continent, simply to visit someone they had once shared a brief, if intensely passionate night with.

Even if he had always regretted that that one night had been all that they had shared.

And now that she knew that Javier was not his grandfather? What difference would that make? Just who was she making a play for here? His throat seemed to close up at the thought that she might actually have used him to reach his grandfather. A job first and then...

'I'm sorry,' Martha said again and this time it seemed that she was saying sorry for something else entirely.

Her fingers flexed under his. Perhaps she was only wanting to ease the strands of her hair from where they had snagged on his face; perhaps she was trying to free her fingers from his too-tight grip that betrayed too much. But it didn't feel like that. To Carlos, already stretched too tight with tension, too viscerally aware of the call of her body to his, it felt too much like a caress. A stroke of the soft tips of her fingers over his already too sensitised skin. The awakening of tiny aftershocks of reaction along every nerve. The uncoiling of something hard and hot and primitive low down in his body. Gnawing at him until he felt raw with need and on the brink of being unable to fight any more.

And it was too much. He'd had enough. No more.

'Don't be sorry,' he snapped, deliberately making himself focus only on the first possible meaning of what she had said. 'I'm not. That's how it is—and I can't see that anything is going to change it.'

And swinging away from her, he launched himself into a dive into the pool, welcoming the cool splash of the water over his face and head as a way of calming him down, bringing him back to reality—and to sanity, he prayed. He pushed himself into action, swimming hard and fast down the length of the pool again and again, never pausing until he was gasping for breath and his arms and legs felt like lead. Only then did he allow himself to let his feet sink to the bottom of the pool so that he could stand up, dashing the water from his eyes.

She'd gone, *gracias a Dios*. The poolside was empty, with no sign of the tall, curvy body that had driven him to such distraction. Martha had gone inside, no doubt driven away by his sharpness, his tart retort. It was what he had wanted and he was relieved to see that he was at last alone. But at the same time there was an uncomfortable nagging sensation deep inside, one that made him shift uncomfortably in the water and then, knowing he couldn't quite drive it away so easily, plunge back into the cool clear depths. In spite of the fact that his muscles were protesting, his heart thudding, he pushed himself harder and harder until finally his body screamed in exhaustion. While he was punishing himself physically he knew some sort of mental peace. But as soon as he came to a halt again, forced to it by sheer physical enervation, the same thoughts, hot and hungry and dangerously disturbing, all came flooding back again no matter how hard he tried to drive them away.

It didn't help that Martha had been partly right, that she had understood so much of why he was here. Javier had summoned him and, hoping against hope for some sort of reconciliation, he had come at the old man's call like some well-trained dog looking for a reward. Coming back had been a mistake—a big one. All it had done was to reinforce the fact that El Cielo was not his home any more and would never be the same again. He no longer belonged here in the place that had once been his security, his foundation, and that made every waking moment in this place an agony of loss.

And finding Martha Jones settled here like some gorgeous sensual serpent in what had once been his personal Garden of Eden only made everything so much worse.

CHAPTER SEVEN

MARTHA was reading on the veranda. Or, rather, she was trying to read. She'd brought a book out here, knowing that she had to wait for Carlos to come back. That she couldn't go to bed, let alone sleep, until she had talked to him. After the scene by the pool, she had known that she couldn't let another night go by without telling Carlos just why she was here. If she'd needed anything to stiffen her resolve that he had the right to know about his child—which she didn't—then the way he had expressed his feelings about family, about the need to belong, had been twisting in her conscience ever since.

She also felt really bad that he felt he had only been summoned here by Javier because of her. Sadly, it seemed it was true, but she could only hope that when Carlos realised that the old man was concerned about the baby they had created between them, then perhaps it might ease the feeling of being unwanted for himself. She prayed it might.

It would help if she could have found Carlos, told him that she wanted to talk to him. But he had been out all day, disappearing even before she had finished getting Javier his breakfast, and she hadn't seen him since. He hadn't come in for the evening meal either. Probably just as well because Javier had been in a difficult mood, fussing and complaining about everything. It had been a relief when he had decided that he wanted to get to bed early.

'So this is where you are.'

Carlos's voice coming through the silence of the night made her start, jumping in her seat so that the book fell from her hands and landed on the veranda with a thud.

Quick footsteps of booted feet sounded on the wood, and the next moment he was kneeling before her, but only to pick up the book and hand it back to her.

'I'm sorry, I didn't mean to frighten you.'

'It's OK…'

She'd planned to say more, that she hadn't really been frightened, but in the moment that she looked down into his dark, shadowed face, met the green flame of his eyes, every other thought fled from her mind. All she could think of was how close he was, how the light from the covered lanterns that provided the illumination out here changed his face, making it look both stunningly beautiful on the side that caught the direct beam of their glow, and shockingly dark and dangerous on the one that fell into the shadow.

'Thank you,' she managed, her voice husky with the need she was powerless to hide. 'You missed lunch— dinner too,' she added, knowing she was only speaking to fill the silence, and recognising from the look on Carlos's face that that was exactly what he was thinking too. 'Where have you been all day?'

'Out with the horses.' It was almost tossed away, but she was so sensitive to him now that she caught the other tones that threaded through it, giving it a very different emphasis. 'Two mares are ready to foal, and there are a couple of yearlings who needed exercise. They obviously haven't been taken out often enough.'

'Javier has tried...' Martha began.

'But he clearly can't manage everything like he used to,' Carlos inserted when she hesitated. 'And I know the animals, as he took care to point out.'

'Did he ask you...?' Martha couldn't hold back on her surprise. She expected, and got, the slightly rueful shake of Carlos's dark head.

'You know my grandfather. He'd rather slit his own throat than ask for help.'

And Carlos had stepped in without being asked, taking responsibility for the *estancia* even though it was no longer part of his inheritance. She noted the slip of the tongue, the way that even now he couldn't always remember that Javier was not actually his grandfather.

'Where is the old man now?'

'Javier's gone to bed. He said he was tired.'

'And if he admitted that then it's more than he would ever acknowledge before. You're good with him—he does as you tell him, lets you help. You can get away with things that would have my head bitten off, chewed up and spat out.'

With her reflections of just moments before still in her thoughts, Martha's smile was touched with melancholy.

'Perhaps it's because I'm a woman—and I'm not family.'

'I'm not family, remember.' It was ragged at the edges, making her heart twist inside her.

'You're the closest thing he's got. And we're usually hardest on our families—on those we love. Because we feel they will take it—out of love.'

'Really?'

Carlos pushed himself to his feet in a rush, taking several long, restless strides across to the other side of the veranda to lean against the high wooden rail that surrounded it.

'And you think that Javier is hard—that he disinherited me—threw me out—out of *love*?'

The black cynicism made her wince painfully. She wanted to reach out to him, touch him—to bridge this gap between them. But she didn't dare do that until she had told him the truth about why she was here. And she feared that when she did tell him the gap between them could only be wider than ever before.

'I know that it hurts you so much because you love him—in spite of what he's done.'

'And I suppose you're now going to tell me that he called me back here out of love too?' Carlos tossed back. 'That it has nothing to do with you?'

'No…'

How she wished she could honestly say it had nothing to do with her being here—for his sake if for nothing else. But it would not be the truth and he would know it if she tried to pretend. Besides, she knew that honesty was the only possible way forward.

'I thought not!'

'But it's not the way you think,' Martha rushed in, unable to take any more of the brittle darkness of his tone. 'It's nothing to do with me making a move on Javier—or on you for that matter. Really it's not.'

She had his attention now. Silhouetted against the darkening sky, his long body was just a darker shape in the shadows, his face almost hidden from her. But she knew from the quality of total stillness, the stiffening of the long, powerful frame, that he was listening intently.

'So what has it to do with?'

'You—and me—and that night in the hotel. The night we met.'

Her throat had dried terribly, her voice failing her so that that 'we met' was just an embarrassing squeak, but one that provoked no trace of laughter from her or the man whose silent focus was directed straight at her face.

'That night,' he repeated, pushing her to go on.

'That night we—the protection didn't work—we— I'm pregnant. I'm having your baby.'

The words fell into the sort of appalled silence in which Martha almost felt that she could hear as well as feel all the tiny hairs on the back of her neck lifting in a rush of terrible awareness. She had never meant to let it out so fast or so unrehearsed. She had fully intended to lead up to it carefully, explain calmly and, she hoped, unemotionally just why she was here. Now she'd gone and blurted it out in an uncontrolled rush. She couldn't have made a bigger mess of it if she'd tried.

Carlos hadn't moved. If anything he was even more frozen than before.

'Baby,' he said, making the single word sound appalling. Martha's blood ran cold just to hear it. 'How the hell did this happen?' Carlos questioned harshly.

'Oh, the usual way!' Martha flung at him, and knew that flippancy was exactly the wrong move when she saw the dark scowl that snapped his black brows together. 'The condom split—it must have. I swear to you it's your baby. You know I was—'

'I know.' His hands came up in a gesture that dismissed what she had been about to say. 'For my sins, I know you were a virgin.'

Well, that gave her the message of the way he was feeling loud and clear—'for my sins'. He'd started pacing again, the restless movements betraying only too clearly the state of his thoughts.

'And I know that the condom split. Why the hell do you think I needed to get out of there—get some air?'

Which spoke volumes for the sense of revulsion he'd felt at the thought that he might one day be faced with just this situation.

'You knew!' Martha's voice was thin with shock. 'But you didn't say anything—you just got out of there—fast!'

'I'm not proud of myself,' Carlos acknowledged. 'I should have handled it so much better. I told you, I expected that you would be there when I got back. I thought we could talk then.'

'And then what? You'd have got down on one knee and told me not to worry, that if I was pregnant, you'd stand by me—no, I thought not,' she added, seeing the new darkness of his eyes. 'Of course not.'

He'd come to a halt, standing before her, and never before had he seemed so tall, so big, so dark. Never before had she been so aware of him as a man, as her—once—lover, as the father of her child.

'No. But I would have wanted to sit down and talk—decide what we would do if there were any consequences from the mistake we made.'

That put it in perspective—perfectly, Martha reckoned miserably. She had been thinking of their baby, a child that she already loved even though it barely existed, of telling him that he was going to be a father. And he—he had been defining it in terms of *consequences*—and *mistakes*.

'Well, consequences happened.' She wished she could wipe that brittle flippancy from her voice but it was the only way that worked to keep the turmoil of emotions she felt inside at bay.

'You are definitely pregnant?'

'Definitely. Four months, three days and—' she glanced at her watch and was disturbed to find that she couldn't read anything on the face of it because hot tears were filming her eyes, blurring her vision '—five hours—give or take a few time zones. It is your baby, Carlos,' she added, suddenly afraid he might not believe her. She had no proof, after all.

'There was no one else?'

'No one!' Indignation sharpened the words. 'What do you think—that I had a long line of men just queuing up? You have to be joking! After the way Gavin behaved—and then you—I really felt that I'd had enough of making a mess of relationships, for a good long while.'

'Do not lump me in with the bastard you were engaged to.' That had really struck home, making his eyes blaze in rejection . 'Whatever else I am, I am not a cheat and a liar like him. And I know you were a virgin when we slept together.'

For my sins...

'I could ask you to take a test,' Carlos stated flatly.

'You could,' Martha agreed, knowing she'd been prepared for this. It was the least she'd expected. 'And I'd do it. I have nothing to hide.'

Those shadowy green eyes had locked onto hers, seeming to probe right behind hers, reaching into her heart, her soul, to find the truth. She didn't know quite what it was that convinced him, or when, but suddenly he nodded just once, sharply, and straightened up again, pushing his hands into the pockets of his jeans.

'Then I believe you. You couldn't be so confident if you were lying. And I'd see it in your face. So, there is a child—my child—and you came here looking for me in order to...'

'To tell you about the baby. And only that.' She was still feeling slightly light-headed at the way that he hadn't really questioned that the baby was his. After the fight she had expected, it had hit like a blow to her head. 'You have a right to know.'

'And then what did you expect me to do?' His frown was puzzled, disbelieving, and the way he held his long body taut and tense spoke of the restraint he was imposing on himself, the distance he was putting between them.

'To do? Nothing.'

She'd expected nothing. Hoped maybe. When he'd come back to El Cielo perhaps she'd allowed herself to dream just a little. But he had showed her no sign that could feed that hope. She could still see the heat in his eyes when he looked at her; heat that showed he still wanted her sexually, but there had been nothing he had said or done that had given any sign that he wanted more than that.

'You can't expect me to believe that.'

'Why not, Carlos—because virgins cling? Well, not this virgin. I came to tell you that we had created a new life between us. A life that I intend to love and care for as best I can. If you want to be part of our baby's life then we'll work something out. Otherwise I'll do this on my own.'

'I've decided I do want a DNA test,' Carlos said abruptly, and because she couldn't see his face the roughness of his tone seemed to scour off a layer of skin that she needed to protect her at this sudden change of heart.

'Of course.' She fought not to show the disappointment that sliced through her. Of course it couldn't have been that easy for him to trust her. What else had she expected? 'You will want to know for definite that the baby is yours... No?' she asked in bewilderment as he shook his dark head in vehement denial.

'No.' The rough tone was so strong, so strangely positive that it sent shivers skittering over her skin in spite of the warmth of the evening. 'I want this child to know for certain who its real father truly is. From the beginning of his or her life. There will never be any doubt, any risk of a sudden discovery that will explode into its life, taking everything he or she believed was real and shattering it.'

As had happened in his life. He didn't have to say the words. There was no doubt as to what he meant. And remembering the way he had watched Javier on the first night, the shock on his face at seeing the old man in the wheelchair, Martha felt new tears—tears that were there for a very different reason—burn at the backs of her eyes.

'And then we will be married.'

It came so quietly, almost an understatement, that for the space of a couple of uneven heartbeats Martha wasn't even sure she had heard right. But as soft as his voice had been it had also been totally obdurate, leaving no room for argument.

But that wasn't how it was supposed to go. It had never been the reason why Martha had come here, come looking for him. How could it be with that savage 'Virgins cling… They have stars in their eyes—and dreams of Prince Charming and happy ever after' still echoing inside her head? She hadn't come here with dreams of a happy ever after. And Carlos could never be Prince Charming—if only because the Prince had been as desperately in love with Cinderella as she had been with him.

And after Gavin, she had no intention of ever opening herself up to any marriage that wasn't securely based in the heart, in love, and not on other, baser needs.

Carefully she drew in a deep breath, nerving herself to find the right words.

'That's not going to happen,' she managed, and was relieved to find that her voice was surprisingly steady, barely a tremble on the words.

'Why not?' If he had been still before, then it was nothing compared to the way he froze now, totally immobile.

'Because we're not getting married.'

CHAPTER EIGHT

'WE'RE not?'

There were so many emotions in those two words. Disbelief, rejection, an edge of anger, stubbornness, but above all total incredulity at the fact that she could possibly be opposing the decision he had made, refusing to go down the path he had determined they would follow.

'No...' She'd managed firmness once, but now all the strength had left her voice and it was barely a whisper. 'We're not.'

'Why the hell not?' It was fiercer this time, harsher.

'Because—because...'

Oh, dear heaven, how could she answer him? What could she say that didn't involve stars in her eyes and Prince Charming and dreams of happy ever after? What could she say that didn't bring in the four letter word—L.O.V.E.?

'I would have thought that as a child who grew up in a one-parent family, you would want your baby to have a mother and a father...'

But not like this. Not when it was only a marriage of convenience—of legality—and she knew it would make Carlos feel trapped because it was something he had never wanted. Because it was just what he had most dreaded when he had realised she had been a virgin on the night they had met.

'Parents don't need to be married to love their child—to share in its upbringing. Your mother and father were married but it didn't stop her from betraying him. My father never even wanted to stay around until I was born… Besides, you and I—we have nothing…'

'Nothing?' Carlos echoed in a way that made her heart catch, stopping the breath high up in her throat. 'How can you say that?'

He moved so quickly that she was sure she hadn't even time to blink and suddenly he was back, crouching before her as he had been just a few minutes—a life-time—ago. He took her hands, stroked his long fingers over them, once, twice, and immediately it was as if the night sky were filled with wild, burning meteorites that flared in front of her eyes.

'We have so much together…' Even in the growing shadows of the evening the burn of his eyes reached her skin, setting it aglow. 'We have this…'

The soft, seductive murmur was somehow so much more compelling, more frightening than the ice of anger that had laced his words moments earlier. All the more so because of the struggle that she had with herself to resist it.

'We're good together,' he told her, supremely confident.

'In—in bed.'

'And surely that's the best place to start?'

To start perhaps, but with nothing else to add in then it was going nowhere. They were going nowhere.

But then she looked down into his face and for the space of a frozen heartbeat she was jolted back in time to that night four months earlier when she had first met this man. When, as Diablo—her devil—he had knelt at her feet on a rain-soaked road and ripped away the confining skirt of her wedding dress so that she could climb onto the motorbike and travel with him away from the ruins of what was supposed to have been her marriage.

She had felt then that she would go anywhere in the world with him in that moment and the truth was that very little—be honest, Martha, *nothing*—had changed. With his darkened eyes locked with hers, his long, lean body almost touching her legs, the scent of his skin tantalising her senses, she felt the heat rising in her blood all over again. She had wanted this man so desperately that first night, and, heaven help her, she wanted him still.

Martha was unable to resist the temptation to reach out, touch the black silk of his hair, even longer than before and blown loose around his face. Emboldened by the way that he made no move to repulse her touch, she let her fingers trace over the width of his forehead, down across his temple, following the forceful line of his jaw. Once again the rasp of stubble against her skin made her nerves quiver and the combination of rough hair and smooth skin sent tiny electrical pulses out and towards the sensitive spots of her body, making her nipples tighten, heat melting like warm honey between her legs.

When he turned his head slightly, twisting to press his warm mouth against the soft inner skin of her wrist, his kiss a torment of sensation, she felt her heart kick sharply in her chest, her breath snatching in and tangling right in the centre of her throat so that she gasped aloud in response.

'I know.' Carlos's voice was low and intent, the sound all the more disturbing when she could only see one half of his face. 'We've been here before.'

'It's very different now,' she managed inanely, that knot in her throat making it almost impossible to speak. 'And—and you—won't be able to rip away my skirt quite so easily...'

The words dried completely as she saw the light catch on the gleam in his eyes and knew that he was thinking very definitely in the present and not of that past night they'd shared.

'Is that what you want me to do?' he questioned softly, his eyes dropping to consider the soft blue ankle-length cotton skirt she wore. 'Because it doesn't look so very difficult to me...'

'I...' Nervously Martha slicked her tongue over lips that had suddenly dried. 'No...' she whispered.

'At least say that in a way that convinces me.'

His voice was pure enticement and the smile that had suddenly warmed his mouth was a wicked temptation she was struggling to resist. She could remember how that mouth had felt on her lips, on her skin, on her breasts and she wanted—needed—to experience it all

over again, her body flooding with scorching awareness and arousal at just the thought.

'Right now you sound as if yes means the opposite—
and no…'

Sliding the book she still held to one side and dropping it onto the floor, he ran one finger lightly over the
cotton of her skirt, lingering at the seam where the two
sides of it were stitched together. And she knew that,
like her, he was recalling just how easily he had ripped
apart the seam of her wedding dress.

'In that voice, no means yes.'

'I…' she tried again, unable to give her voice any
strength.

She knew what she should be doing, what she should
be saying. Carlos in an unexpectedly softer mood like
this was a rare opportunity. She should be telling him
why she could never marry him—why she didn't need
to marry him. But telling him would also be a way to
ruin this new, approachable mood. To risk turning it
into a white blaze of fury or an icy cold rejection. And
she didn't yet feel quite ready to do either.

'If it's any help to you, I totally understood why you
behaved as you did that night.'

'You did?'

Martha was grateful for the way that the shadows of
the evening hid the rush of blood that she could feel rising in her cheeks, knowing that otherwise they would be
glowing bright pink. He'd switched on that smile again
so that she felt that she was melting in its warmth. And
she definitely didn't want to lose that.

Carlos nodded his dark head.

'You had planned to lose your virginity that night but circumstances conspired against you. That must have been so frustrating. You wanted things to change but—'

'I wanted things to change so I grabbed at any passing man?' Indignation burned, making her fling the words into his upturned face. 'Any port in a storm? Don't insult your—don't insult my intelligence—it wasn't like that at all!'

'No?' Carlos shifted slightly, moving to kneel at her feet, rather than crouch beside her. 'Then tell me—what was it like?'

'It was…'

Dared she tell the truth? Or was it worse to hold it back? She only knew that she couldn't bear to have him think that he had been nothing more than an itch she had desperately needed to scratch. What they had shared had been something really special. At least for her. It had been the wedding night she would have wanted if she had ever had a wedding to a man she loved.

A terrible shockwave of disbelief shuddered through her as she realised just what had been in her mind. In her thoughts she had been picturing Carlos as the groom with whom she had wanted to spend her wedding night. Carlos as the man she had connected with the word…

'What was it like?'

'Like this…'

She was trying to block out her own thoughts every bit as much as answer his question, Martha knew. The need to do so pushed her forward, pressing her mouth against his, taking his lips in a wild embrace that had them opening under the pressure of her assault and he gasped slightly, his breath mingling with hers.

'I met a man who affected me like no other had ever done before. A man I wanted to kiss and touch...'

She suited actions to the words, hearing him drag in a raw, uneven breath as she did so.

'Who I wanted to touch me. A man I felt I'd been waiting for all my life. The man who could teach me what it meant to be a woman. And strangely, unbelievably, he seemed to want me too.'

'Strangely?' The word seemed to be choked out of Carlos, half groan, half laughter. *'Querido Dios,* woman, have you seen yourself? You're beautiful— gorgeous.'

'G-Gavin never thought so.' There, she'd made herself admit it, found the courage to face it.

'Then the man's a bigger fool than I already knew he was.' The way that Carlos shook his head so vehemently washed away the memory under the impact of his words. 'Does the idiot have no eyes as well as no brain?'

'I feel beautiful when I'm with you,' Martha acknowledged, feeling the warmth of joy flood her veins, sing in her head. 'I felt gorgeous that night. Because you wanted me as much as I wanted you. You made me feel like I was the only woman in the world.'

'You were the only woman in the world for me that night.' His voice was rough, coming apart at the edges. 'I wanted you then and I want you now.'

'Oh, yes.'

It was a sigh of recognition, of acceptance, of consent. And it was the consent he acted on, surging to his feet and taking her with him. He had turned things around now so that it was his mouth plundering hers and that was how she wanted it. Returning kiss for kiss, she clung to him as he lifted her from the lounger, her arms flung up around his neck, her hands tangling in his hair. He half walked, half carried her inside and up the back stairs, away from Javier's personal suite, heading for the rooms that Martha had prepared for him only a couple of days before.

On every second step he paused, crushing her against the wall to kiss her harder, press his body along the length of hers so that the heat and force of his erection seared into her skin through the soft fabric of her clothes. But even that was too much of a barrier, putting a distance between the real heat of skin on skin, which was what she really wanted.

Somehow, stumbling, awkward, snatching at kisses, grabbing at each other, never looking where they were going, they made it to his bedroom. Hurried steps took them across the room, tumbling them down in a heap of limbs and kisses onto the bed. In spite of the way her hands were shaking in reaction, Martha managed to pull up the polo shirt he wore, find the warm satin of his waist, his stomach. And from the moment they touched every last restraint vanished in a wild explosion of fire and hunger that couldn't be controlled.

Clothes were wrenched off, ripping in the process, tossed onto the floor. Kisses were wild and fierce and harshly demanding, as uninhibited as the touches that were nothing like a caress but more an incitement to frenzy, to hunger, to taking pleasure wherever and however they could find it. There was nothing of finesse or caution in their lovemaking, only a yearning need that had them coming together in a storm of sensation, a powerful surge of want that had Martha arching back and crying aloud in the moment that he pushed into her, hard and strong and, oh, so hot in his possession of her.

Her fingers clutched at the power of his shoulders, nails digging into the corded muscle that bunched and flexed under her hands. She was soaring higher and higher, losing herself completely, but never losing him, so that she knew the moment that he abandoned himself to the ecstasy that crashed over him, throwing herself after him just a couple of wild, keening heartbeats later.

In the moments between bliss and reality, as she slowly sank back to earth, Martha knew nothing but the heat and strength of Carlos's arms around her, the wild thudding of his heart just under her ear. Like this, right here and now, everything was perfect. There was no need of words, because all the communicating they had done had been on the most basic, primitive level. If only it could stay like this, without the complications of language that could be misunderstood or taken the wrong way. If only...

Beside her Carlos stirred, sighing deeply, muttering something in thick rough Spanish under his breath. In another world she might have thought—have hoped—that he was thinking along the same lines as her, that he too wished that everything could always be as simple as the basic communication of their bodies, with nothing else ever having to be said.

But the truth was that really, deep down, even that communication hadn't been simple or straightforward. Because when she knew exactly why she had felt so powerfully passionate towards Carlos just now, she had no idea at all how he had truly felt about her. He had wanted her. That was all he had said. His body had been so very involved in what had happened—there had been no mistaking that. But what about his mind? His heart? She had no answer for those questions and knew that as soon as she asked them then the complications had started up again and she was lost on a sea of uncertainty, not knowing where it might take her.

A sigh that almost matched his escaped her and slowly Carlos turned to look at her, green eyes sensually sleepy with the look of a man who had just sated a burning physical hunger.

'It's all still there, isn't it?' he said softly. 'Every bit as powerful as it was before. Nothing has faded, nothing has weakened. There's just you and me—and this inferno that flares between us every time we touch. And that's what will make our marriage worth having.'

'Just you and me,' Martha echoed, forcing herself to erase the note of longing from her voice. Just for a moment, she was almost tempted to go back and reconsider his marriage proposal—marriage declaration—emotionless as it had been. If only there were just her and Carlos, no one else to consider.

And that thought brought her upright in a rush of shock at the memory of the fact it could never be just her and Carlos ever again. That there was always someone else who had to be considered in all this. The baby.

'What is it?' Her movement had alerted Carlos, making him lift his head, stare at her through narrowed dark eyes. 'What's wrong?'

What was wrong? If he needed to ask then how could he ever understand her answer?

He clearly thought that he had just convinced her that a marriage based on glorious sex and nothing else would be enough. *She* knew that it could never be that way—that it would take too much from her, leave her just an empty, lonely shell, and ultimately it would destroy her. She had to tell him why marriage to him would never work, why she had to reject his proposal, but she didn't know how. Didn't know where to begin.

CHAPTER NINE

SHE couldn't just launch into it, cold and raw. She had to lead into this carefully and—she hoped—gently.

Pushing a hand through the fall of her blonde hair, she stared at the wall opposite, not brave enough to look into his face. Not yet.

'Virgins cling,' she said uncertainly, quoting the words he had used at their first meeting. 'Why did you say that? What makes you think—?'

'I don't think; I know,' Carlos put in sharply, moving restlessly against the pillows. His impatient tone told her that he didn't think this topic relevant to what had just happened.

'Why?' Martha asked. 'What happened? Who was it who made you feel that way?'

From the way his face closed up, heavy lids dropping down to hood over his eyes, she felt sure he wouldn't tell her. But then he shrugged one shoulder, dismissing the importance of her question—or of his memories.

'I was just eighteen—at college. I met a girl.'

He looked away, stared out of the window at the outline of the mountains away in the distance, pink-tinged with the setting sun.

'I was just looking for some fun and I thought that was what Ella wanted too. She was a year older than me and I assumed she was already experienced. She wasn't.'

Carlos raked one hand through the darkness of his hair in a gesture that betrayed his unease.

'I made the mistake of breaking up with her very soon after but she believed herself in love with me. She also thought that I should be in love with her—and wouldn't take my word that was not how I felt. She made my life hell—hounding me, refusing to let me go. She had a key to my rooms and I would come home at night and find her in my bed. She told everyone who would listen how appallingly I'd treated her, threatened to slash her wrists. She even turned up at El Cielo—one night she cut herself and claimed that I'd done it to her...'

Martha's indrawn breath, the way she had swung round to face him, unable to believe what she was hearing, made him glance back at her, mossy green eyes clouded with memory.

'She said it was because she was in love with me. Perhaps she was...'

'No.' Martha was shaking her head furiously. 'That's not what love does to people. Love makes you want what is best for the other person, want them to have what they need. Trailing after someone like that—hounding them—threatening—trying to ruin their life—that's stalking.'

Message to self, she noted in the privacy of her own thoughts. This was exactly what she needed to remember. This was why, even if he pressured her to accept a marriage that deep down inside Carlos never really wanted but was only offering because of his sense of responsibility towards their baby, she had to say no. She had promised herself that she would never cling. That she would go, leave him in peace, to live his life with the freedom he needed. That was the way it had to be...

Her thought processes stopped dead at that point and she stared blankly into the distance exactly as Carlos had done. And this time she felt that, like him before her, she wasn't seeing any of the beauty of the lake, the proud range of the mountains bathed in the warm rosy glow of the setting sun.

Even if she loved him, she recognised when her mind recovered from the blow that shock had dealt it. Even though she loved him, which she now realised that she did. Totally and completely. At some point over the past few days, perhaps even before that, she had lost her heart to Carlos Diablo—Carlos the devil—who had come into her life so shockingly and unexpectedly and now seemed to have taken it over, filling a hole that she had never even realised was there, making her realise that love was so much more than a need for security, the wanting to be loved that had deceived her into thinking she could marry Gavin.

What a fool she had been. Experiencing the wild rush of emotions, the burn of desire, the achingly hungry yearning that just being with Carlos made her feel, Martha suddenly thought she understood something of what had been going through this Ella's mind. But she also knew that she would stand by her own opinion, no matter what it cost her. If he didn't love her back then there was no way she would hound him, make him feel the desolation the other girl had brought into his life. If she couldn't have his love then there was no way she was going to risk making him hate her as he must surely have hated Ella all those years ago. So much so that he still lived by the rule that her behaviours had created in his mind. They couldn't work together in the future if he hated her. And they were going to have to work together if only for the baby's sake. There was no way that she was going to have her child made a victim of a tug of war between his parents.

Turning so that she was even closer to Carlos, her head almost touching his, her hair draping like a curtain over his face, she looked deep into his eyes.

'That wasn't love—it was obsession. And stalkers don't want love. They want possession.'

Something had happened. She saw the flicker of a change in his eyes, the shift of muscles in his face.

'I was afraid of what she might do,' he said, so softly that for a moment she was unsure of whether she had heard him right. But the echo of his words was there in his expression, in the way the muscles were drawn tight across his bones, his mouth a rigid line of control so that she saw how it had cost him to make the admission. 'That she might ruin what I had with my grandfather—the only family I had.'

'Oh, Carlos…'

He laughed, a harsh, bitter sound that made her wince deep inside and when he spoke again she knew that the moment of weakness, of openness, was gone and he had once more retreated behind the mask of not giving a damn.

'Turns out I need not have worried. I never had a relationship with my grandfather to destroy. My mother managed to deal the death blow to that one.'

The mother who hadn't wanted him for himself but had dumped him on Javier and gone off to live her own selfish life.

If she had needed any more convincing that she was doing the right thing, then it was there in those words, in the bitter laughter that did nothing to convince her he was actually feeling any amusement. Carlos was still the man who didn't do happy ever after—and who could blame him with the experience of his mother's and then Ella's behaviour scarring him emotionally?

'Some relationships are just not worth having,' she said now. 'Real love doesn't trap people, it sets them free to be themselves.'

Softly she touched her lips to his, not knowing if it would be what he wanted or not. But as soon as their mouths met she felt the change in his heartbeat, the uneven break in his breathing. One long arm hooked up around her neck, pulling her down on top of him so that he could kiss her fully, strongly, her mouth opening to him, her body crushed against his.

'Enough talk,' he muttered. 'Enough. There are better ways...'

His hands were on her now, stroking, caressing, arousing the hungry yearning she had only known since the day she had met him. She had felt desire before, but she had never known this fury of passion, which overrode all the safe, civilised rules by which she'd once tried to live her life. It was frightening, and thrilling at the same time, and her response was every bit as blatant as his desire. Any words, any more complications would only stop this, take it from her. And she needed to know it, if only for one more time.

How could she deny herself this for tonight? The truth and all its complications would have to be faced before very long. But for now, this was all she wanted. And for now it was enough.

So she gave herself up to the hunger that boiled like lava inside her, let it erupt and overflow, taking her thoughts and mind along with it, leaving her with only feeling. And this man who had somehow become the entire world to her in such a short space of time.

Tomorrow would be another day. Tomorrow she would tell him again that she couldn't marry him, and she would have to try to convince him of that when all the time her own foolish heart would be longing to accept his proposal, such as it was, and to hell with the consequences.

But first she would have just one more night.

CHAPTER TEN

That's not going to happen... Because we're not getting married.

We have nothing...

Carlos urged his horse into a faster pace, heading out into the open country, miles from the *estancia*, feeling the powerful chestnut respond swiftly to his lightest touch. In the past it had been at times like this, out in the wilds, with only the animal for company, that he had been at his most content. He could ride for miles, free and uninhibited under the soaring blue skies, clear his mind to deal with whatever was worrying him, and then finally head back to El Cielo feeling so much more at peace with the world.

He'd dealt with problems this way even as a child, but then on a much smaller pony that his grandfather had given him as a birthday gift. Back in the days when he had believed that Javier was his grandfather. He remembered riding for miles and miles on the day they had told him that his father was dead, not returning home until he was too tired to ride any further, dropping out of the saddle from sheer exhaustion as he reached the main door of the big house. And again when the letter informing him that his mother had recently remarried and her new husband didn't want the child from her first marriage living with them had arrived on his tenth birthday.

In the end he'd grown accustomed to being on his own. He and his 'grandfather' had rubbed along well enough even if the old man found it hard to show affection or even a hint of warmth. But their shared passion for the polo ponies that were bred on the *estancia* and for El Cielo itself gave them some connection. And El Cielo was the only home he'd known; the one link with his father.

Until he'd learned that his father was not his father at all and had lost home, parent and his identity all in one blow. Leaving him not knowing who he was.

I would never have known who you really are. Which was what you wanted in the first place, wasn't it? The words Martha had flung at him sounded in his mind.

Who *was* he really? What would have been the point in telling her anything when he didn't know himself? Wasn't that why he had come here when Javier had summoned him? He had been fool enough to hope for a reconciliation but he had had no idea what had changed the old man's mind.

Except that now he did know. Javier hadn't changed his mind at all. Instead he had only summoned Carlos here to do right by Martha Jones.

If he had had any doubt about that then the way that Javier had talked to him today, the things he'd said, had made it only too plain.

'Maldita sea!'

Carlos tossed the curse into the blue arc of the sky, letting the horse gallop where it wanted, not focusing at all on where they were heading.

He had tried to 'do right' by Martha. Martha and his child. It was all he wanted to do—to do the right thing, to care for them. To make sure that his baby did not grow up as he had done, not knowing who it was or where it belonged. He wanted that child to know that there was one place it belonged. With him. With its father and mother. Its family.

Family. He had only the vaguest memory of what being in a family meant. There were shadows in the back of his mind that reminded him of when he had been a child, not yet nine, when he and the man he had believed was his father had lived here at El Cielo. The memories weren't clear but the feeling was. The feeling of being loved, being secure. Of belonging.

He wanted that for his child. He and Martha could do that between them. She would be a brilliant mother, he had no doubt about that. The way she was with Javier showed that, the easy way she dealt with his demands and tempers, her patience, her care.

But Martha had refused to marry him.

We have nothing...

How could she say they had nothing when they had nights like last night? Nights that had burned with pleasure, long, long hours lost in the enjoyment of each other. And then the final exhausted collapse into the depths of sleep, wrapped in each other's arms. How could that be *nothing*?

And even better, what could compare to the moment

of waking, of knowing that she was still there, sleeping beside him, and with the prospect of the rest of the day—the rest of their lives—to do the same?

How the hell could that be *nothing*?

And not just the sex. The time to be together, to talk, to laugh, just to be together. He had left her asleep when he had woken in the early hours of the morning, and already he was missing her. Never, on any of the rides he had taken in the past, had he ever missed anyone. And it had started on that night they had met.

He had tried to walk out of there too before he got in too deep, but he had found that he couldn't just walk away from her. He had had to go back to her and when he had found that she was no longer there he had been unable to forget her. The truth was that he was in too deep already.

She had said that she was pregnant with his child, and he had believed her instinctively. That was so shocking that it had rocked his sense of reality. And it had held out to him the prospect of something that he had never considered how much he wanted until now. Coming back to El Cielo and realising it was no longer home had made him realise what he most wanted in all the world.

A home. A family. A place to belong.

'Some relationships are just not worth having.' Martha's voice sounded so clearly inside his head that for perhaps the first time in years—since he had been that nine-year-old boy—he tugged on a horse's reins, causing the chestnut to throw up its head. 'Real love doesn't trap people, it sets them free to be themselves.'

Was that how she felt? Trapped in a relationship with him because of the baby? But she had come to his bed so willingly—given of herself so generously. His blood heated hotter than the early morning sun at just the memory.

Or did she mean...?

Carlos eased up on the speed of the chestnut, restraining it carefully as it gradually slowed from its racing gallop to a walk. The wild ride that might have eased his feelings, concentrated his attention in the past no longer seemed to have the sort of effect that he was aiming for. He couldn't outrun or distance himself from everything he'd left behind because the emptiness would always be there. The only time it went away was when he was with Martha.

He turned the horse back towards where El Cielo stood against the mountainside, its cream painted walls washed in brilliant sunlight. He'd talked to Javier and got one set of answers. Now he needed to face Martha, confront her with a whole new set of questions. And the answers to those had the power to change his life for ever.

Martha put the last of the laundry into the washing machine and closed the door, sighing as she switched the machine on. She had managed to hold things together while she had plenty to keep herself busy, but now, with every task on her list done, and Javier dozing in his chair in his sitting room, she was left with nothing to distract her from the fact that Carlos seemed to have vanished from El Cielo.

She knew that her time here on the *estancia* was coming to an end. She had done what she'd come here for. She'd found Carlos, told him about the baby, and if she was lucky then he might want to be part of the child's life in the future. But that was all. She had no intention of accepting Carlos's unilateral declaration—because she could hardly call it a proposal—that they were to be married. She hadn't escaped one loveless marriage to Gavin only to tie herself into another, particularly when she knew that one day, inevitably, Carlos would feel trapped and hate her for it. He might think that the baby was reason enough right now, but without love there was nowhere for any marriage to go.

She knew this was the truth in her heart, but still she quailed at the thought of trying to persuade Carlos that it was so. His anger and rejection would be hard enough to take, but if he turned on her the gentle seduction that he had used during the night, the soft words and even softer enticing kisses, then she didn't know if she was strong enough to resist him.

In fact—determination fired her, stiffening her spine and lifting her chin—she was so sure she knew how Carlos would react that she was best to accept that now and start preparing for the rest of her life. If she packed her things, she would be ready to leave, just as soon as she had talked to him. Even though it tore at her heart, she had to accept that if he didn't love her there was no future for her with him. She would cope on her own. And she would have the birth of her baby to look forward to. A child that would be a constant reminder of the man she adored.

She was in her room, folding clothes ready to put them in her case, when she heard the main door open and the sound of hard, forceful footsteps downstairs.

'Martha!' Carlos's voice echoed around the big hallway and up the stairs and the dark thread of something carefully controlled in it set her nerves on edge.

For a moment she considered keeping quiet, not sure she wanted to risk the coming confrontation with him in this mood. The meeting was going to be uncomfortable but only then could she hope to go forward into her future with a clear conscience.

'Up here!' she called to him.

The rapid thud of his feet on the stairs sounded like a drumroll of doom and Martha's hands tightened on the dress she was folding, crushing it terribly. A moment later the door to her room was pushed open, and the dark figure of Carlos appeared in the doorway.

Except that today he wasn't Carlos Ortega. The man who stood so close and yet so very far away was once more the dark and disturbing Diablo, the man she had met on the isolated English road on the stormy, wet day that had changed her life. Something twisted sharp and deep in her heart at the memory as she took in his windblown, dishevelled hair, the casual clothing of jeans and a tee shirt combined with long leather riding books that were well worn and spattered with dust. He had clearly been outside for some time and the glow of the sun was on his handsome face.

But not in his eyes. There was no warmth in the mossy green depth, no light of any kind. They were dead in a way that she had never seen before. She had seen him angry, intrigued, amused, flirtatious and—oh, dear heaven, she had seen him seductive and in the throes of burning passion. But she had never seen this terrible distance, completely cut off from her as if he had surrounded himself with ten-foot-high walls with not a single chink in them, no hint of softening at all. What had she done to make him look this way?

'You could at least knock,' she snapped, nerves getting the better of her.

'Perdón,' he returned tartly, and with a disturbing twist to his beautiful mouth he gave a sort of ironical bow, and, lifting a hand, rapped his knuckles three times on the wooden panel of the door.

'Better?'

'Perfect, thank you.'

'I thought we had got past all that…'

'We slept together—that doesn't give you the right to trample in where you're not—not invited.'

It was ridiculous to sound so stiff after the night of heated sensuality they had just shared but there was so much else in her mind that she couldn't find a way to pitch her tone at the right level. This man who looked like Diablo—was she really fool enough to think of him as 'her' Diablo?—but was someone else entirely than the knight on a powerful motorbike, was suddenly a stranger all over again and she didn't know how to handle him.

Except that she knew she had to tell him that she was leaving.

Tears stung at the backs of her eyes at the thought of going. She had nerved herself to leave Carlos, but to be confronted by the Diablo of her memories, the man who had come to her rescue and who had given her such a wonderful night of pleasure, made her feel that she would never find the strength to go. But he didn't love her, and she had vowed already that she would never cling.

She had just psyched herself to speak when Carlos got there first.

'I asked you to marry me last night.'

'It was hardly asking!' Martha had to point out. 'As I recall you made a statement—"We will be married," was what you said. I don't remember having any choice in the matter.'

'It seems the logical way to proceed.'

'For you maybe, but I don't happen to think that marriages should be based on logic or procedures— not when they result from your "sins", and in order to legalise the "consequences" of your mistakes.'

'That isn't the only reason I suggested marriage and you know it!'

The flare of something dangerous in his eyes told her just how much her words had hit home and for a moment she almost regretted them.

'I want to be part of my child's life,' he said roughly— so roughly that it stunned her. This was something new. She had never heard that frayed-at-the-edges tone on Carlos's tongue before now.

'Of course—we can talk about that.'

'We'll talk about it now.'

Martha's hands tightened on the dress she was fold-ing, creasing it badly. She had always known they would need to discuss access, but the darkness of his frown, that adamant tone, worried her. Was she going to have to fight him over this?

'You can have all the access you want...' she began, but he was shaking his head even before she had finished the sentence.

'You know I don't want to be a part-time father. I don't want my child to grow up as I did, barely knowing its parents—with one of them on an entirely different continent. I want—'

'You want!' Martha couldn't hold back any more. 'You want—what about what I want? I grew up in a one-parent family. I wouldn't wish that on my child if I could help it.'

She saw her mistake too late, saw the way that his eyes narrowed sharply before he pounced on what she had said.

'There is an easy way to make sure that doesn't happen.'

Martha focused her attention on the dress again, trying to smooth out the creases and add it to the pile already collecting on her bed.

'It might be easy for you but it isn't for me.' She only found it possible to say it because she wasn't looking at him, didn't have to see the anger, the rejection in his eyes.

'What does that mean? To me it's perfectly simple.'

It was so simple it was terribly complicated. Martha fussed with a tiny detail of the dress, unfastening and refastening a button, to hide the distress that she knew would show in her face if she lifted her head.

She needed love before she could commit herself to marriage; Carlos did not. He saw marriage purely as a legal arrangement—one with sexual benefits—while she wanted to see it as the joining of two hearts and two lives to make a single whole.

Two totally opposing beliefs that created a vast unbridgeable chasm between them and because of that...

'Is your answer still the same?'

'Yes.'

What other response could she make? Lifting her head, she faced him as bravely as she could, her chin coming up defiantly, her eyes stretched wide and unblinking as she fought against the tears she was determined not to let him know were there.

'I mean—no—I can't—won't marry you. It wouldn't work between us.'

'Why not?'

'Oh, please don't ask me that!' Martha's grip on her control was weakening.

And if he pressed her with another 'why not' on that then she felt that she would shatter completely, and end up telling him how much she longed for his love. It was only the image of how he would react to that emotional declaration that stilled her tongue. It would be the perfect example of the sort of virgin *with stars in her eyes and dreams of Prince Charming and happy ever after* that he so hated.

'I'm not going to marry you—I just want you to be part of our baby's life. Be there for him or her, be a real father, love it—that's all I'm asking of you.'

It was what she would have thought Carlos wanted

too. To be a father to his child and keep his freedom. So why had he suddenly gone so very silent? Why had his long body stiffened as if in rejection and withdrawal? Martha took a couple of steps towards him, stopping reluctantly when that stone-eyed glare warned her to stay away. It was only then that she realised she had actually lifted her hands, wanting to reach out to him, but that gesture too froze uncompleted.

'That's *all* you're asking for?'

How did he make that sound like some sort of accusation, as if she had flung the worst possible insult in his face?

'Yes. Yes, it is.'

'And you are determined to manage on your own? But I can— You don't even have a job, or a home. You'll need some help.'

'I'll be fine.'

'At least let me give you financial support. No?' he questioned as Martha shook her head firmly.

'No. Carlos, the truth is that I want nothing from you—unless you want to offer it. I don't need your support because I have money of my own—lots of it.'

CHAPTER ELEVEN

'You have...'

The shock on his face was so total, so disbelieving that, suddenly finding that her legs were strangely unsteady underneath her, Martha moved to sink down onto the bed, grateful for its support.

What had she expected? she asked herself. That his astonishment at her refusal to agree to marry him, all those questions, that intensity had meant that he was heading towards a very different sort of offer? That he might have actually been going to say...

Had she really been fool enough to think—to hope— that he was leading up to a declaration of love? She would have to be crazy to even dream of that. But still the confirmation of the fact that he was only offering financial support seemed to drain the blood from her head so that she felt nauseous and faint as she had in the very early days of her pregnancy.

'That—that was why I was getting married, in fact— though I didn't realise it at the time. I won over seven million on the lottery,' she explained when she saw his frown of confusion. 'Gavin knew about it, but when he proposed to me I thought it was because he loved me.

It was only on the morning of the wedding that I found out...'

'That he was screwing your bridesmaid.'

Carlos remembered how appalled she had looked when she had told him that, the pain that had burned in her eyes. That was when he'd begun to realise how much she'd got to him. The sympathy he'd felt for her pain. The rage at the snake of a fiancé who'd betrayed her.

She'd got in under his radar somehow and he hadn't known how to handle it. And then when they'd had sex...

'You have money?'

He was struggling to get his head round this. She had refused to marry him, how many times could he ask and get the same single-word response— *No*? She wouldn't be his wife, have his name, let him be at her side. She wanted him to be a father to their child but nothing to *her*.

The offer of money had been the last resort. Something he could give her that surely she would benefit from. It would make her life easier. But she had money of her own.

If she had money for herself then what would she ever need from him? And somewhere, deep down in his soul, he knew how much he wanted her to need him. To need him as he needed her.

'So—when you came here looking for me...'

'Did you really think that I only came because of your wealth—that the size and luxury of El Cielo and everything else you own were what had brought me here?'

He deserved the accusation in those beautiful eyes, felt the sting of it mixed brutally with guilt deep inside. He could even feel the burn of embarrassed blood in his cheeks and didn't care. He deserved her anger and she deserved to know how bad he felt about it.

'I was a fool even to consider it. I should have known that the woman who left a bundle of notes in a hotel room to help what she believed was an impoverished traveller with nothing but what he stood up in pay the cost of the night there could never be just a gold-digger. It was an insult to you. I'm sorry, Martha. I apologise unreservedly that the thought ever crossed my mind.'

Martha blinked slightly, her soft eyes glazed with an unexpected sheen as she nodded her blonde head rather brusquely.

'Thank you for that. The only reason I ever came here was to tell you about the baby. And now that I have...'

She was getting to her feet again and the movement made her breasts sway under the loose-fitting tunic top. Her fuller, more evident breasts. He had noticed that when he had first seen her again. Noticed—and liked it—but how could he have not put two and two together right there and then?

Because he had been knocked way off balance by the realisation that she was here. And by the thought that she was settled at El Cielo with Javier. He'd told himself that it was El Cielo that mattered. He'd even tried to convince himself that she was working something on Javier, but deep down he'd known it was something else—that he was jealous of her presence here. And that had made him behave so very badly.

'Now I'm going.'

She was picking up something from the floor, the dress she had dropped a moment or two before, the movement giving Carlos a heady eyeful of her rich hips, the firm tight globes of her bottom. His body's instant response, hardening fast and hot, made it difficult to think straight. But he had to think. Last night he had simply reacted—and that had got them precisely no-where.

'Going? No way!'

The look she turned on him was one of disbelief, of rejection of his protest. And now, too late, he saw that as well as the growing pile of clothes on the bed there was also a case—standing open and half filled. She was already on her way out of here. She'd told the truth when she'd said she didn't need him.

But he needed her.

'Oh, come on, Carlos, what else do we have left to say?'

What did they have left to say? There must be some-thing he could say that would make her stop, make her reconsider her determination to leave.

'I talked to my grandfather. He says that he's changed his mind and he wants to leave me El Cielo.'

It was out before he had time to think if it was wise. He saw the amazement hit her face as the already crum-pled dress dropped to the floor again. The unconcealed joy in her expression lit her up from within, the grey eyes even more brilliant as her beautiful mouth curved into a wide, unrestrained smile.

'He did? Oh, that's wonderful. So that's why he summoned you back here. No?' she questioned as he shook his head slowly.

'No.'

Her smile faded, the slightly melancholic curve to her full lips making him want to take her in his arms and crush those soft lips under his own. But now was not the right time. In fact he was beginning to wonder if there ever would be a right time again. He had barely had time to absorb the news that she was having his baby...

His child...

His gaze went to the curve of her hips, the line of her soft belly. Somewhere in there, his child was growing. The child he had never allowed himself to think that he might want but now... Oh dear heaven, now....

A family of his own. The family he had never had and always wanted. The realisation that he had come so close to this made his head spin. But there was another thought that acted like the splash of icy water in his face and brought the harsh lash of reality with it.

So near and yet so far. Because the other thing that Javier had said could make the dream impossible when he revealed it to her.

'But El Cielo should be yours—like you said, you worked so hard for this place, you helped to build it up.'

'And, of course, there is no one else.'

He knew he sounded disillusioned. He was disillusioned. With the memory of the way he had felt when

Javier had offered him what he had once thought was his dream come true in his thoughts, he could no longer feel anything else. In the moment Javier had made his announcement, all he'd been able to think of was the realisation that it was no longer his dream—that another bigger, more vital hope had taken its place.

'That is why Javier has decided to leave it to me—because he saw how I cared about the place. And because I know the horses—the breeding stock—he thinks that I will continue to make the place a profitable enterprise if I'm in charge. And of course the profits from this place have always been so important to him.'

'I don't understand— If Javier leaves it to anyone, it should be to you.'

But there was where the problem lay, Carlos acknowledged privately. Because the conditions under which El Cielo had been offered were such that he could never ever accept. Not if he ever wanted that family—a real, true family—with Martha and the baby.

She had turned back to the packing again and it was all that he could do not to stride forward and snatch the clothes from her hands, tell her she was going nowhere.

'I said no!' he blurted out, needing this said. Needing her to know.

Martha shook her head in confusion. 'Why?'

'I said I can't accept the inheritance.'

'Can't?' she questioned. 'Don't you mean won't?'

'Well, yes, I won't—because it would be wrong.'

That stunned her, her head going back in shock, her eyes widening.

'How can it be wrong?'

'Because if I accept Javier's offer then I can never ask you to marry me again.' He spoke slowly, clearly, needing her to really take this in. It was the most important thing he had ever said. 'And I do plan on asking you again and again and again—every opportunity I get until I get the answer I want from you. But if I accepted Javier's terms then I could never prove that I was marrying for the right reasons.'

'And those reasons are?' Was that rough, hoarse voice really hers? Martha wondered. She sounded as if she'd swallowed a packet of razor blades.

'Because I've met someone who's changed my life. Someone who makes me feel—makes me think of a future when before I was trying to get away from the past. Someone who can offer me a new—a real—identity, rather than the one I thought I had and then lost. And that identity means that I am a father to my child, part of a real family—the sort I never thought I'd know.'

Someone who's changed my life. Someone who makes me feel—makes me think of a future... A real family. It sounded so wonderful that she felt tears burn at her eyes again. But she had to remind herself sharply that Carlos was talking in ideals. That these were the real reasons he would want to marry someone—the reasons he wouldn't marry her because she wasn't the person who made him feel that way. Vaguely she became aware of the fact that Carlos had said something more, something she hadn't caught, and the rather uncomfortable laugh that accompanied the words jolted her out of her thoughts.

'What did you say?'

Carlos's eyes met hers and she saw a strange blend of sincerity and an embarrassed amusement in their green depths.

'I said did you know how many Miss Joneses there are in the north of England?'

'But why—you were looking for me?' She couldn't believe it but it was the only possible explanation.

'I couldn't just let you walk out of my life like that. I should have stayed, talked, told you about the condom—asked what you wanted to do for the future if we needed to. Instead I gave in to a moment of weakness. I was furious with myself for not being able to resist you. I'd been able to do it before, with other women—been able to say no. But with you...I couldn't say no to you. And I was so shocked by my own behaviour—by my weakness—that I had to get out of there and clear my head. I just assumed you'd stay—I was a fool. If you knew how I felt when I got back to that room and found you gone—leaving that money.'

With a rough, revealing movement he raked both hands through the jet darkness of his hair, pushing it back from his face so that she could see the sincerity that was stamped onto his stunning features.

'I wish you'd stayed.' There was no doubting the sincerity in his face, in his voice, and it shook Martha rigid.

'You do?'

Slowly he nodded his dark head, those moss-coloured eyes seeming to draw her in deeper and deeper with every breath she took. Was this really happening? Could he truly be saying...?

'I was running when I met you. Running from things I didn't want to face, things that changed my whole perception of who I am. You made me want to stop. I didn't know who I was—but with you that didn't matter any more. With you I was just the traveller with only what I stood up in. With you I could just *be*.'

'I wanted to stay.' She offered it hesitantly. 'But I was determined not to cling.'

His reaction was unexpected. A smile, the first genuine smile he had offered her since he had marched into her room with all the marks of strain and doubt stamped onto his face. Those marks had gone now, she realised, the very last of them smoothing out in that smile.

'Damn it, did you not think that perhaps I *wanted* you to cling? That if you'd still been there when I got back we could have had a chance to talk—to make that the start of something. Instead I came back to an empty room—a discarded dress—and a bundle of notes on the tray. And I had no way to find you.'

'You—wanted to find me?'

He nodded again. 'I went back to the place we met—on that road. The one clue I could find was that you had been holding—planning on holding your wedding near there. When I saw that hall nearby then I knew it had to be the right one. I got your address—but by the time I found your flat you'd already gone, leaving it in the hands of the estate agents.'

'You came looking for me?' She still couldn't take it in. She had thought that he had wanted her out of his life and so she'd gone. But what did this mean?

She couldn't stop her mind going back to the things he had said a moment before.

You made me want to stop. I didn't know who I was... With you I could just be.

And even earlier: *Someone who's changed my life. Someone who makes me feel—makes me think of a future.* That sounded an awful lot like...

'Carlos...' she tried but her use of his name clashed with his voice.

'I want you in my life, Martha—I have done from that first day we met. I didn't know what had hit me, only that something had done. Hard. I reacted the way I did—walking out like a fool—because I was appalled at my own lack of control—and the fact that the condom breaking might mean that it would force you to stay with me.'

There was that laugh again, the rough-edged, self-derisory sound that she wanted to kiss away from his mouth.

'It took me a long time to realise that what I was feeling was the beginning of love, Martha, but I'm getting there now. I just didn't recognise it then. All I knew was that I didn't want you to feel any sort of coercion—any sort of pressure. I wanted you to be with me as I wanted to be with you.'

'I do.'

Her response caught him by surprise, making his head go back in shock. The green eyes were so deep and dark that she felt she could lose herself in them and in the message they were giving silently.

'I want to be with you, Carlos—and not just because

of the baby. I want you. And I hope you can see that the fact that I have my own money—that I don't need you for that—means that I want *you*. Just you. The man you are—the man you were—that traveller who appeared on the road beside me with nothing but what he stood up in…'

She didn't get any further because Carlos had moved forward, reaching for her and gathering her up into his arms, holding her tight against him. His mouth came down hard on hers, kissing away doubts, offering hope—and most of all speaking so eloquently of that love that he had been stumbling over expressing just moments before. Martha clung to him as she kissed him back, putting all of herself, her heart and all that was in it into her own expression of love without words.

'I have something to tell you,' he said at last when the storm of feeling had ebbed for the moment and they were sitting side by side on the bed, her hand in his.

Something important, his tone told her, and her heart jolted in nervous anticipation. He'd said he couldn't marry her if he accepted Javier's bequest to him. So was there something more he hadn't told her?

'Javier said that I could have El Cielo—but only if I married you. I had to do right by you, make you my wife so that our child was born legitimate—and then he'd put me back into his will.'

Carlos nodded sombrely, his mouth stiff with something he was still holding back.

And now she understood the tension that had simmered in him when he had walked into the room earlier. He had felt that he was trapped, caught by the two people he wanted to love and who should have loved him. He hadn't known for sure that she loved him.

'I understand,' she said softly, squeezing his hand tightly to drive home her point.

'I know you do.' Carlos's smile was slow, gentle, as he returned the pressure threefold. 'And so you'll know that I can't take El Cielo. I don't want it—not like this. Not if I hope to marry you. Because I do so want to marry you and have my own family but if I take my grandfather's conditional bequest then how will you ever know that I want you for the right reasons—because I want you and our child and nothing more? I want it to go back to how it was that day when we met. Just the two of us and what we stand up in—and our baby.'

Another kiss, sweeter, surer than the first took away any remaining worry that Martha might have felt. Looking up into his beloved face, she placed her hands on either side of his head and gazed deep into his eyes, seeing everything she needed right there.

'It was when Javier laid out his conditions that I knew,' Carlos said, looking deep into her eyes. 'I felt so repulsed by what he was doing—had to reject it outright without a second thought. Because in that moment I knew that everything you've taught me was true.'

'Everything *I've* taught you?' Martha's voice almost broke on the words. She couldn't believe she had had such a huge effect on this man.

'Oh, yes,' he assured her. 'You've shown me that family doesn't come from blood or from a name or even from a place you think is home. It's not what you own, what you inherit—a family is built on nothing like that—a family is nothing but love. And love doesn't have terms and conditions, rules and regulations attached to it—it just is. Javier can't buy my love, even with El Cielo, and I don't need the *estancia* or anything else to make me love you. Because I do love you, Miss Jones—I love you with my heart, my soul, with every breath that's in my body. And I want to marry you because of you—and not because of El Cielo or anything else in the world.'

'Don't condemn Javier too harshly,' she said softly, needing to give him back some hope on this. 'It might just have been that olive branch you hoped it was.'

'I know. He might just, like me, have come to realise that the ties of love are far stronger, far richer than the ties of blood. But I still can't take El Cielo if it would mean that there was any doubt in your mind about the way I feel for you.'

'Nothing could make me doubt that now,' Martha assured him, knowing it was true. 'I want to marry you too, Carlos. And I am totally sure that you will marry me for the right—the best of reasons. Because you love me.'

If he would give up something that had meant so much to him for so many years—the loss of which had sent him out on that cold, wet, lonely road on which they'd first met— If he'd give that up for her, then how could any doubt even enter her thoughts, never mind her heart?

'Real wealth isn't measured in money. Or land,' Carlos said between kisses that drifted over and over her face as if he could never kiss her enough to express the love that he felt for her. 'All we need is us—and our baby. El Cielo might be a heaven on earth but if it comes at too high a price then it's just not worth the cost. With you I have everything. With you I have the world and without you I have nothing.'

'We'll create our own family, our own home—and fill it with love,' Martha told him. 'We'll have the world to share together.'

Guiding his hands gently, she laid them on her womb, on the child they had created together, and saw the look of awe and joy spread over his face.

'We have all that we need right here, my love. All that matters. We'll build our own heaven together for the future.'

* * * * *

CLASSIC

EXTRA

You can find more information on upcoming Harlequin® titles, free excerpts and more at www.Harlequin.com.

HPECNM0412

REQUEST YOUR FREE BOOKS!

Harlequin *Presents*

PASSION GUARANTEED SEDUCTION

2 FREE NOVELS PLUS
2 FREE GIFTS!

YES! Please send me 2 FREE Harlequin Presents® novels and my 2 FREE gifts (gifts are worth about \$10). After receiving them, if I don't wish to receive any more books, I can return the shipping statement marked "cancel." If I don't cancel, I will receive 6 brand-new novels every month and be billed just \$4.30 per book in the U.S. or \$4.99 per book in Canada. That's a saving of at least 14% off the cover price! It's quite a bargain! Shipping and handling is just 50¢ per book in the U.S. and 75¢ per book in Canada.* I understand that accepting the 2 free books and gifts places me under no obligation to buy anything. I can always return a shipment and cancel at any time. Even if I never buy another book, the two free books and gifts are mine to keep forever.

106/306 HDN FERQ

Name	(PLEASE PRINT)
Address	Apt. #
City	State/Prov. Zip/Postal Code

Signature (if under 18, a parent or guardian must sign)

Mail to the **Reader Service:**
IN U.S.A.: P.O. Box 1867, Buffalo, NY 14240-1867
IN CANADA: P.O. Box 609, Fort Erie, Ontario L2A 5X3

Not valid for current subscribers to Harlequin Presents books.

**Are you a current subscriber to Harlequin Presents books
and want to receive the larger-print edition?
Call 1-800-873-8635 or visit www.ReaderService.com.**

* Terms and prices subject to change without notice. Prices do not include applicable taxes. Sales tax applicable in N.Y. Canadian residents will be charged applicable taxes. Offer not valid in Quebec. This offer is limited to one order per household. All orders subject to credit approval. Credit or debit balances in a customer's account(s) may be offset by any other outstanding balance owed by or to the customer. Please allow 4 to 6 weeks for delivery. Offer available while quantities last.

Your Privacy—The Reader Service is committed to protecting your privacy. Our Privacy Policy is available online at www.ReaderService.com or upon request from the Reader Service.

We make a portion of our mailing list available to reputable third parties that offer products we believe may interest you. If you prefer that we not exchange your name with third parties, or if you wish to clarify or modify your communication preferences, please visit us at www.ReaderService.com/consumerschoice or write to us at Reader Service Preference Service, P.O. Box 9062, Buffalo, NY 14269. Include your complete name and address.

HP11B

Harlequin® Romance

Award-winning author

DONNA ALWARD

*brings you two rough-and-tough
cowboys with hearts of gold.*

CADENCE CREEK
COWBOYS

They're the Rough Diamonds of the West

From the moment Sam Diamond turned up late to her
charity's meeting, placating everyone with a tip of his Stetson
and a lazy smile, Angela Beck knew he was trouble.

Angela is the most stubborn, beautiful woman Sam's ever met
and he'd love to still her sharp tongue with a kiss, but first
he has to get close enough to uncover the complex woman
beneath. And that's something only a real cowboy can do....

THE LAST REAL COWBOY
Available in May.

And look for Tyson Diamond's story,
THE REBEL RANCHER,
coming this June!

Stop The Press! *Crown Prince in Shock Marriage*

When Crown Prince Alessandro of Santina
proposes to paparazzi favorite Allegra Jackson
it promises to be *the* social event of the decade!

Discover all 8 stories in the scandalous
new miniseries THE SANTINA CROWN
from Harlequin Presents®!

***

Enjoy this sneak peek from Penny Jordan's
THE PRICE OF ROYAL DUTY,
book 1 in THE SANTINA CROWN *miniseries.*

"DON'T YOU THINK you're being a tad dramatic?" he
asked her in a wry voice.

"I'm not being dramatic," she defended herself. "Surely
I should have some rights as a person, a human being, some
say in my own fate, instead of having my future decided
for me by my father. To endure marriage to a man who has
simply agreed to marry me because he wants an heir, and to
whom my father has virtually auctioned me off in exchange
for a royal alliance."

"I should have thought such a marriage would suit you,
Sophia. After all, it's well documented that your own chosen lifestyle involves something very similar, when it comes
to bed hopping."

A body blow indeed, and one that drove the blood from
Sophia's face and doubled the pain in her heart. It shouldn't
matter what Ash thought of her. That was not part of her
plan. But still his denunciation of her hurt, and it wasn't one

EXP0412

she could defend herself against. Not without telling him far more than she wanted him to know.

"Then you thought wrong" was all she could permit herself to say. "That is not the kind of marriage I want. I can't bear the thought of this marriage." Her panic and fear were there in her voice; even she could hear it herself, so how much more obvious must it be to Ash?

She must try to stay calm. Not even to Ash could she truly explain the distaste, the loathing, the fear she had of being forced by law to give herself in a marriage bed in the most intimate way possible when… No, that was one secret that she must keep no matter what, just as she had already kept it for so long. "Please, Ash, I'm begging you for your help."

Will Ash discover Sophia's secret?
Find out in THE PRICE OF ROYAL DUTY
by
USA TODAY *bestselling author*
Penny Jordan

Book 1 of THE SANTINA CROWN *miniseries*
available May 2012 from Harlequin Presents®!

Harlequin *Presents*®

Royalty has never been so scandalous!

THE
SANTINA
CROWN

When Crown Prince Alessandro of Santina proposes
to paparazzi favorite Allegra Jackson it promises
to be *the* social event of the decade!

Harlequin Presents® invites you to step into the decadent
playground of the world's rich and famous and rub shoulders
with royalty, sheikhs and glamorous socialites.

**Collect all 8 passionate tales written by *USA TODAY*
bestselling authors, beginning May 2012!**

The Price of Royal Duty by **Penny Jordan**(May)

The Sheikh's Heir by **Sharon Kendrick**(June)

Santina's Scandalous Princess by **Kate Hewitt**(July)

The Man Behind the Scars by **Caitlin Crews**(August)

Defying the Prince by **Sarah Morgan**(September)

Princess from the Shadows by **Maisey Yates**(October)

The Girl Nobody Wanted by **Lynn Raye Harris**(November)

Playing the Royal Game by **Carol Marinelli**(December)

HPI3066SC